PUFFIN BOOKS

The Puffin Book of Christmas Stories

Wendy Cooling was educated in Norwich and, after a short time in the Civil Service, spent time travelling the world. On her return to England she trained as a teacher, went on to teach English in London comprehensive schools for many years and was for a time seconded as an advisor on libraries and book-related work in schools. She left teaching to work on the promotion of books and reading as Head of The Children's Book Foundation and now works as a freelance book consultant and reviewer.

She has edited many short story and poetry anthologies, including the millennium collection *Centuries of Stories*.

Some other books edited by Wendy Cooling

THE PUFFIN BOOK OF

Christmas Stories

Edited by Wendy Cooling

Illustrated by Nick Ward

PUFFIN BOOKS

PUFFIN BOOKS

Published by the Penguin Group
Penguin Books Ltd, 80 Strand, London WC2R 0RL, England
Penguin Putnam Inc., 375 Hudson Street, New York, New York 10014, USA
Penguin Books Australia Ltd, 250 Camberwell Road, Camberwell, Victoria 3124, Australia
Penguin Books Canada Ltd, 10 Alcorn Avenue, Toronto, Ontario, Canada M4V 3B2
Penguin Books India (P) Ltd, 11 Community Centre, Panchsheel Park, New Delhi – 110 017, India
Penguin Books (NZ) Ltd, Cnr Rosedale and Airborne Roads, Albany, Auckland, New Zealand
Penguin Books (South Africa) (Pty) Ltd, 24 Sturdee Avenue, Rosebank 2196, South Africa

Penguin Books Ltd, Registered Offices: 80 Strand, London WC2R 0RL, England

www.penguin.com

First published 2001
5

The Acknowledgements on pages 169–70 constitute an extension of this copyright page

Set in 13/18 Centaur
Typeset by Rowland Phototypesetting Ltd, Bury St Edmunds, Suffolk
Made and printed in England by Clays Ltd, St Ives plc

British Library Cataloguing in Publication Data
A CIP catalogue record for this book is available from the British Library

ISBN 0–141–30661–0

Contents

CONTENTS

The Christmas Party

(from *A Northern Childhood*)

George Layton

Our classroom looked smashing. Lots of silver tinsel and crepe paper and lanterns. *We'd* made the lanterns, but Miss Taylor had bought the rest herself, out of her own money. Oh, only today and tomorrow and then we break up. Mind you, if school was like this all the time, I wouldn't be bothered about breaking up. Putting up Christmas decorations and playing games – much better than doing writing and spelling any day. I watched the snow coming down outside. Smashing! More sliding tomorrow. I love Christmas. I wish it was more than once a year. Miss Taylor started tapping on the blackboard with a piece of chalk. Everybody was talking and she kept on tapping until the only person you could hear was Norbert Lightowler.

'Look if I get a six and land on you, you get knocked off and I still get another go!'

The whole class was looking at him.

'Look, when Colin got a six, he landed on *me* and *he* got another . . . !'

Suddenly he realized that he was the only one talking and he started going red.

'Thank you, Norbert, I think we all know the rules of Ludo.'

Miss Taylor can be right sarcastic sometimes. Everybody laughed. Even Miss Taylor smiled.

'Now, since it is getting so noisy, we're going to stop these games and do some work.'

Everybody groaned and Tony and me booed – quietly so Miss Taylor couldn't hear. She hates people that boo. She says people who boo are cowards.

'Who is that booing?'

We must have been booing louder than we thought.

'Who is that booing?'

Miss Taylor looked at Tony. I looked at Tony. They both looked at me. I put my hand up.

'It was me, Miss.'

Tony put his hand up.

'It was me an' all, Miss.'

She looked at us.

'You both know what I think of booing, don't you?'

We nodded.

'Yes, Miss.'

'Yes, Miss.'

'Don't ever let me hear it again.'

We shook our heads.

'No, Miss.'

'No, Miss.'

She turned to the class.

'Now, the work I have in mind is discussion work.'

Everybody groaned again, except me and Tony.

'I thought we'd discuss tomorrow's Christmas party!'

We all cheered and Miss Taylor smiled. We have a Christmas party every year, the whole school together in the main hall. Each class has its own table and we all bring the food from home.

'Now, does everybody know what they're bringing from home for the party tomorrow?'

I knew. I was bringing a jelly. I put my hand up.

'I'm bringing a jelly, Miss!'

Everybody started shouting at once and Miss Taylor moved her hands about to calm us down.

'All right, all right, one at a time. Don't get excited. Jennifer Greenwood, what are you bringing?'

Jennifer Greenwood was sitting in the back row next

to Valerie Burns. She wriggled her shoulders and rolled her head about and looked down. She always does that when she's asked a question. She's daft is Jennifer Greenwood.

'C'mon, Jennifer, what are you bringing for tomorrow?'

She put her hand up.

'Please, Miss, I'm bringing a custard trifle, Miss.'

Norbert Lightowler pulled his mouth into a funny shape and pretended to be sick.

'Ugh, I hate custard. I'm not gonna have any of that!'

Everybody laughed, except Miss Taylor.

'Well, Norbert, if I was Jennifer I wouldn't dream of giving you any. Right, Jennifer?'

Jennifer just rolled her head about and giggled with Valerie Burns. Norbert was looking down at his desk.

'And, Norbert, what are you bringing tomorrow?'

'Polony sandwiches, Miss, my mum's making 'em, and a bottle of mixed pickles, Miss, homemade!'

Miss Taylor said that would be lovely, and carried on asking right round the class. Tony said that he was bringing a Christmas cake. I was bringing the jelly that my mum was going to make, and Colin Wilkinson was bringing some currant buns. Valerie Burns said that she was bringing some lemon curd tarts, and Freda Holdsworth called her a spiteful cat because *she* was bringing the lemon curd tarts, and Valerie Burns *knew* she was bringing lemon curd tarts because she'd told her and she was a blooming copy-cat. Anyway Miss Taylor calmed her down by saying that it was a good job they were both bringing lemon curd tarts, because then there would be enough for everybody, and everybody would want one, wouldn't they? And she asked everybody who would want a lemon curd tart to put their hands up, and everybody put their hands up. Even I put my hand up and I hate lemon curd. Well, it *was* Christmas.

After everybody had told Miss Taylor what they were bringing, she said that there'd be enough for the whole school, never mind just our class, but we should remember that Christmas isn't just for eating and parties, and she asked Tony what the most important thing about Christmas is.

'Presents, Miss!'

'No, Tony, not presents. Christmas is when the baby Jesus was born, and that is the most important thing, and when you're all enjoying your presents and parties this year, you must all remember that. Will you all promise me?'

Everybody promised that they'd remember Jesus and then Miss Taylor started asking us all how we were going to spend Christmas. Freda Holdsworth said she was going to Bridlington on Christmas Eve to stay with her cousin, and on Christmas Eve they'd both put their stockings up for Father Christmas, but before they'd go to bed, they'd leave a glass of milk and some biscuits for him in case he was hungry. Norbert Lightowler said that that's daft because there's no such thing as Father Christmas. Some of the others agreed, but most of them said course there is. I just wasn't sure. What I can't understand is, that if there *is* a Father Christmas, how does he get round everybody in one night? I mean the presents must come from somewhere, but how can he do it all by himself? And Norbert said how can there be only *one* Father Christmas, when he'd seen *two* down in town in Baldwin Street and another outside the fish market, and Neville Bastowe said he'd seen one in Dickenson's. Well, what about the one my mum had taken me to see at the Co-op? He'd promised to bring me a racer.

'Please, Miss, there's one at the Co-op an' all. He's promised to bring me a racer.'

And then Miss Taylor explained that all these others are Father Christmas's brothers and relations who help out because he's so busy and Freda Holdsworth said Miss Taylor was right, and Norbert said he'd never thought of that, but that Paul Hopwood, he's in 2B, had told him that Father Christmas is just his dad dressed up, and I said that that's daft and it couldn't be because Father Christmas comes to our house every year and I haven't got a dad, and Miss Taylor said that if those who didn't believe in Father Christmas didn't get any presents, they'd only have themselves to blame, and I agreed! Then she asked me what I'd be doing on Christmas Day.

'Well, Miss, when I wake up in the morning, I'll look round and see what presents I've got, and I'll play with them and I'll empty my stocking, and usually there are some sweets so I'll eat them, and when I've played a bit more I'll go and wake my mum up and show her what I've got, and then I'll wake my Auntie Doreen – she always stays with us every Christmas; and then after breakfast I'll play a bit more, and then we'll have Christmas dinner, and then we'll go to my grandad's and I'll play a bit more there, and then I'll go home to bed, and that'll be the end!'

Miss Taylor said that all sounded very nice and she hoped everybody would have such a nice Christmas, but she was surprised I wasn't going to church. Well, I told her that there wouldn't really be time because my grandad likes us to be there early to hear Wilfred Pickles on the wireless visiting a hospital, and to listen to the Queen talking, and then the bell went for home-time and Miss Taylor said we could all go quietly and told us not to forget our stuff for the party.

I went with Tony to get our coats from the cloakroom. Everybody was talking about the party and Barry was there shouting out that their class was going to have the best table because their teacher had made them a Christmas pudding with money in it! I told him that was nothing because Miss Taylor had given everybody in our class sixpence, but he didn't believe me.

'Gerraway, you bloomin' fibber.'

'She did, didn't she, Tony?'

Tony shook his head.

'Did she heckers like – she wouldn't give 'owt away.'

Huh! You'd think Tony'd've helped me kid Barry along.

'Well, she bought all our Christmas decorations for the classroom . . .' and I went to get my coat. I took my gloves out of my pocket and they were still soaking wet from snowballing at playtime, so I thought I'd put them on the pipes to dry.

'Hey, Tony, my gloves are still sodden.'

'Well put 'em on the pipes.'

'Yeh, that's a good idea.'

While they dried I sat on the pipes. Ooh, it was lovely and warm. There's a window above the basins and I could see the snow was still coming down, really thickly now.

'Hey, it isn't half going to be deep tomorrow.'

Everybody had gone now except for Barry, Tony and me. Tony was standing on the basins looking out of the window and Barry was doing up his coat. It has a hood on it. I wish I had one like it. I could see through the door into the main hall where the Christmas tree was. It looked lovely. Ever so big. It was nearly up to the ceiling.

'Hey, isn't it a big Christmas tree?' Tony jumped down from the basin and came over to where I was sitting.

'Yeh. It's smashing. All them coloured balls. Isn't it lovely, eh, Barry?'

Barry came over.

'Not bad. C'mon you two, let's get going, eh?'

'Just a sec, let's see if my gloves are dry.'

They weren't really but I put them on. As I was fastening my coat, Barry said how about going carol singing to get a bit of money.

Tony was quite keen, but I didn't know. I mean, my mum'd be expecting me home round about now.

'I suppose *you* can't come because your mum'll be cross with you, as usual!'

Huh. It's all right for Barry. His mum and dad aren't bothered where he goes.

'Course I'll come. Where do you want to go?'

Barry said down near the woods where the posh live, but Tony said it was useless there because they never gave you nowt. So we decided to go round Belgrave Road way, where it's only *quite* posh. It takes about ten minutes to get to Belgrave Road from our school and on the way we argued about which carols to sing. I wanted 'Away in a Manger' but Barry wanted 'O Come all Ye Faithful'.

'"Away in a Manger" isn't half as good as "O Come all Ye Faithful", is it, Tony?'

Tony shrugged his shoulders.

'I quite like "Once in Royal David's City".'

In the end we decided to take it in turns to choose. Belgrade Road's ever so long and we started at number three with 'O Come all Ye Faithful'.

'O Come all ye faithful, joyful and trium . . .'

That was as far as we got. A bloke opened the door, gave us three halfpence and told us to push off.

Tony was disgusted.

'That's a good start, halfpenny each.'

Barry told him to stop grumbling.

'It's better than nothing. C'mon.'

We went on to number five and Tony and Barry started quarrelling again because Tony said it was his turn to choose, but Barry wanted his go again because we'd only sung one line. So we did 'O Come all Ye Faithful' again.

'Oh come all ye faithful, joyful and triumphant, Oh . . .'

We didn't get any further this time either. An old lady opened the door and said her mother was poorly so could we sing a bit quieter. We started once more but she stopped us again and said it was still just a little bit too loud and could we sing it quieter.

'O come all ye faithful, joyful and triumphant, O come ye, o come ye to Be—eth—lehem . . .'

And we sang the whole thing like that, in whispers. We could hardly hear each other. I felt daft and started giggling and that set Tony and Barry off, but the old lady didn't seem to notice. She just stood there while we sang and when we finished she said thank you and gave us twopence each.

At the next house we sang 'Once in Royal David's City' right through and then rang the doorbell, but nobody came. We missed number nine out because it was empty and up for sale, and at number eleven we sang 'Away in a Manger'.

We went to the end of the road singing every carol we knew. We must've made about a pound between us by the time we got to the other end, and Barry said how about going back and doing the other side of the road. I was all for it, but I just happened to see St Chad's clock. Bloomin' heck! Twenty to nine! I couldn't believe it. I thought it'd be about half-past six, if that. Twenty to nine!

'Hey, I'd better get going. It's twenty to nine. My mum'll kill me!'

The other two said they were going to do a bit more carol singing, so they gave me my share of the money and I ran home as fast as I could. I took a short cut through the snicket behind the fish and chip shop and I got home in about five minutes. I could see my mum standing outside the front door talking to Mrs Theabould, our next door neighbour. She saw me and walked towards me. I tried to act all calm as if it was only about half-past five or six o'clock.

'Hello, Mum, I've been carol singing.'

She gave me a clout. She nearly knocked me over. Right on my freezing cold ear an' all.

'Get inside, you! I've been going mad with worry. Do you know what time it is? Nine o'clock. Get inside!'

She pushed me inside and I heard her thank Mrs Theabould and come in after me. I thought she was going to give me another clout, but she just shouted at me, saying that I was lucky she didn't get the police out, and why didn't I tell her where I was? By this time I was crying my head off.

'But I was only bloomin' carol singing.'

'I'll give you carol singing. Get off to bed,' and she pushed me upstairs into my bedroom.

'But what about my jelly for tomorrow? Have you made it?'

I thought she was going to go mad.

'Jelly! I'll give you jelly. If you think I've nothing better to do than make jellies while you're out roaming the streets! Get to bed!'

'But I've told Miss Taylor I'm bringing a jelly. I've got to have one. Please, Mum.'

She just told me to wash my hands and face and get to bed.

'And if I hear another word out of you, you'll get such a good hiding, you'll wish you hadn't come home,' and she went downstairs.

I didn't dare say another word. What was I going to do about my jelly? I had to bring one. I'd promised. There was only one thing for it. I'd have to make one myself. So I decided to wait until my mum went to bed, and then I'd go downstairs and make one. I don't know how I kept awake. I'm sure I nodded off once or twice, but after a while I heard my mum switch her light out, and when I'd given her enough time to get to sleep, I crept downstairs.

I've seen my mum make jellies tons of times and I knew you had to have boiling water, so I put the kettle on. I looked in the cupboard for a jelly and at first I thought I'd had it, but I found one and emptied it into a glass bowl. It was a funny jelly. Not like the ones my mum usually has. It was sort of like a powder. Still, it said jelly on the packet, so it was all right. A new flavour most likely. I poured the hot water into a bowl, closed the cupboard door, switched off the light, and took the jelly upstairs and I put it under my bed. I could hear my mum snoring so I knew I was all right, and I went to sleep.

Next thing I heard was my mum shouting from downstairs.

'C'mon, get up or you'll be late for school.'

I got up and pulled the jelly from under the bed. It

had set lovely. All wobbly. But it was a bit of a funny colour, sort of yellowy-white. Still I'd got my jelly and that's what mattered. My mum didn't say much when I got downstairs. She just told me to eat my breakfast and get to school, so I did. When I'd finished I put my coat on and said tarah to my mum in the kitchen and went off. But first I sneaked upstairs and got my jelly and wrapped it in a piece of newspaper.

The first thing we had to do at school was to take what we'd brought for the party into the main hall and stick on a label with our name on it and leave it on our table. Norbert Lightowler was there with his polony sandwiches and mixed pickles. So was Neville Bastowe. Neville Bastowe said that my jelly was a bit funny-looking, but Norbert said he loved jelly more than anything else and he could eat all the jellies in the world. Miss Taylor came along then and told us to take our coats off and go to our classroom. The party wasn't starting till twelve o'clock, so in the morning we played games and sang carols and Miss Taylor read us a story.

Then we had a long playtime and we had a snowball fight with 2B, and I went on the slides until old Wilkie, that's the caretaker, came and put ashes on the ice. Then the bell went and we all had to go to our tables in the main hall. At every place was a Christmas cracker, and everybody had a streamer, but Mr Dyson, the Headmaster, said that we couldn't throw any streamers until we'd finished eating. I pulled my cracker with Tony and got a red paper hat and a pencil sharpener. Tony got a blue hat and a small magnifying glass. When everybody had pulled their crackers we said grace and started eating. I started with a sausage roll that Neville Bastowe had brought, and a polony sandwich.

Miss Taylor had shared my jelly out in bowls and Jennifer Greenwood said it looked horrible and she wasn't going to have any. So did Freda Holdsworth. But Norbert was already on his jelly and said it was lovely and he'd eat anybody else's. Tony started his jelly and spat it out.

'Ugh, it's horrible.'

I tasted mine, and it *was* horrible, but I forced it down.

'It's not that bad.'

Just then Tony said he could see my mum.

'Isn't that your mum over there?'

He pointed to the door. She was talking to Miss Taylor and they both came over.

'Your mother says you forgot your jelly this morning, here it is.'

Miss Taylor put a lovely red jelly on the table. It had bananas and cream on it, and bits of orange. My mum asked me where I'd got my jelly from. I told her I'd made it. I thought she'd be cross, but she and Miss Taylor just laughed and told us to enjoy ourselves, and then my mum went off. Everybody put their hands up for a portion of my mum's jelly – except Norbert.

'I don't want any of that. This is lovely. What flavour is it?'

I told him it was a new flavour and I'd never heard of it before.

'Well, what's it called?'

'Aspic.'

'Y'what?'

'Aspic jelly – it's a new flavour!'

Norbert ate the whole thing and was sick afterwards, and everybody else had some of my mum's. It was a right good party.

The Silver Horse

Ursula Moray Williams

Christmas Eve and stars in the sky! Snow, snow everywhere, and the wide white world so quiet!

Inside the carpenter's shop six wooden hobby-horses stood beside the work bench, waiting for Santa Claus. One red, one blue, one green, one yellow, one purple and one white with spots, they all had round black eyes and scarlet wheels, of which they were very proud. Old Mr Tandy the carpenter had just finished making them.

Now he was tidying up his shop before going down the village street to eat a mince pie and drink a cup of tea with old Mrs Higgins. The Christmas bells were ringing. In two hours it would be midnight and he wanted company.

Far away across the fields came the galloping hooves of a silver horse. It was the Christmas horse with a bag on its back, gathering up the naughtiness the children had thrown away before Santa Claus came.

All the children had said their prayers and begged pardon for their badness during the year. Now they were fast asleep in bed with their stockings hung up, smiling in their sleep.

The Christmas horse came galloping down the street to stick his head over the half-door of the carpenter's shop.

'Oh, you beautiful thing!' cried the hobby-horses, clattering to welcome him.

'I can't stay to play with you!' said the silver horse. 'I have hundreds of miles to go! Happy Christmas to you all! Goodbye!'

Away he went down the village street.

'What a pity!' said the hobby-horses, listening to the flying feet.

The smallest of the hobby-horses had nibbled a hole in the bag on the back of the silver horse. He wanted to find out what was inside it. And something had got out!

There in the snow where the silver horse had stood was a small round creature with bright eyes and turned-out toes. It was a bundle of badness belonging to Little Mikey.

Little Mikey was a boy who always ran away. He ran away from home, he ran away from school. When Christmas time came he made up his mind never to run away again. He had said he was sorry and thrown his naughtiness out of the window. Now it had escaped out of the bag on the back of the silver horse.

'Come out and play!' said Little Mikey, dancing in the snow.

'No! No! No!' said the hobby-horses.

'Just a little frisk in the fields! Just a little gallop in the snow!' said Little Mikey. 'Hark at the Christmas bells! There's lots of time before Santa comes! Come out with me!'

'No! No!' said all the hobby-horses. 'Old Mr Tandy would be very angry!'

'He wouldn't know!' said Little Mikey. 'Come out and try your scarlet wheels! Come out and stretch your wooden legs! Come out and jump in the snow and slide on the ice!'

'No!' said the hobby-horses.

'Then I shall go after the silver horse,' said Little Mikey, 'but now I shall never catch him up! I have wasted my time talking to you and I shall be left behind and never see him again, unless one of you lets me ride on your back, but of course not one of you is as fast as he!' and the little creature began to sniff.

The hobby-horses came trotting out of the workshop. They were sorry to see Little Mikey sad, and every one of them wished to prove that he could catch up with the silver horse. The leader took Little Mikey on his back and they galloped like the wind up the quiet village street.

Old Mr Tandy the carpenter was just finishing his cup of tea.

'What was that?' he said to Mrs Higgins. 'The Christmas horse has already gone by and it is still too early for Santa Claus. I had better be getting back to my workshop!'

But when Mr Tandy got back to his workshop the door was wide open and the hobby-horses were gone! The poor old carpenter sat down with his head in his hands and cried.

Presently he wiped his eyes and blew his nose. 'Crying won't bring back my horses!' he said. 'I had better go and find them!'

He took a stick to walk with and a lantern off the peg to light his way. Then he tramped off up the village street to follow the hobby-horses and the silver horse.

Presently he had left the village behind, with all the lighted windows lit up by spangled Christmas trees. Frosty fields and woods stretched out before him, with snow-filled ditches and frozen streams.

The hobby-horses had left the road, and now their tracks led over hill and dale. They had jumped over hedges and leaped over ditches, and among the trails left by their scarlet wheels were the sharp clear hoof-prints of the silver horse.

Now and again Mr Tandy stooped down to pick up a fragment of broken braid, a wisp of mane torn by the branches, or even a battered wheel. Once he found a whole bridle hanging on a hedgerow, and the snow was stained with splinters of painted wood.

Old Mr Tandy tramped for miles, but he knew he would never catch up with the silver horse. Presently he turned round, and began slowly and painfully to make his way home again. His lantern went out, and his stick was broken, so he had to throw it away.

Half an hour before midnight he stumbled through the door and sat down to dry himself before a fire of wood-shavings. In a few minutes he was fast asleep.

Outside, the white world was quiet again under the snow, until far away across the fields came the galloping hooves of a silver horse. And with the galloping a tappeting and clattering as if wooden sticks were tapping and wooden wheels going round.

Nearer and nearer they came till they clattered down the village street. The workshop door was pushed open and the hobby-horses trotted in. Outside in the snow stood the silver horse whinnying a piercing whinny.

Old Mr Tandy woke with a start, and the first thing

he saw was his six hobby-horses. But oh! what a state they were in! Their wheels were broken, their paint was scratched, their manes were torn and their legs were battered. And every one of them hung his head in shame and penitence. The silver horse had a hole in his bag and out of the bag were sticking the runaway legs of Little Mikey.

Old Mr Tandy did not stop to scold them. With his needle and thread he quickly stitched up the hole in case anything else should escape and cause mischief. Then he gave the silver horse a kindly clap on the back and away it galloped till the sound of its hooves could no longer be heard, while Mr Tandy set to work mending the reins and painting the legs and hammering new wheels on his hobby-horses, faster than he had worked in all his life before.

Two minutes before midnight the job was done, and only one thing was missing. The pretty red wheels they had all been so proud of had been replaced by plain white wooden ones. That was their punishment, and it would remind the hobby-horses never to run away again.

As the last wheel was fixed, the Christmas bells began to peal with a new and joyful sound, mingling with the tinkle of sleighbells and the patter of reindeer's feet.

Mr Tandy took his hobby-horses to the door. Then he kissed each one on the nose and stood waiting for

Santa Claus and listening to the Christmas chimes across the sparkling snow, while the reindeer sleigh came nearer and nearer, and far, far away across the wide white world beyond the village galloped the silver horse.

Just Like an Angel

GILLIAN CROSS

Gabriel was the youngest in the family, and he wasn't like his brothers. Michael, Richard and Edward were long-legged and cheerful, with blond hair and blue eyes, but Gabriel was small and shy. The others teased him about everything.

Especially angels.

It started when he was four. They were on their way to stay with Grandmother, for the Christmas carol service. As they drove into her village, Gabriel looked out of the car window and saw big, white shapes circling in the sky. They were moving slowly, with the winter sunlight glancing off their wings.

They weren't aeroplanes. Gabriel knew that aeroplanes moved faster, and made a noise. He lifted his hand and pointed.

'Look! Angels!'

Michael and Richard and Edward fell about laughing.

'Hey, Mum! Gabe thinks those are *angels!*'

'Leave him alone,' Mrs Jennings said. 'They're gliders, Gabriel. Like aeroplanes without engines. They ride on the air currents.'

Her voice was kind, but she was laughing too. She couldn't help it. As they drove up the main street of the village, she stopped at the petrol pumps, and told Mr King the garage man, speaking slowly and clearly, so that he could see what she was saying.

'Gabriel thought the gliders were angels.'

Gabriel shrank back into the car, waiting for Mr King to laugh. But he didn't. He stroked his long beard thoughtfully and smiled into the car.

'Funny you should say that. I often think the same thing, when I'm up in my glider. *Just like being an angel . . .*'

Suddenly, Gabriel didn't feel stupid any more. He sat up straight, and smiled back at Mr King. And his brothers leaned out of the car windows, calling out in loud, clear voices.

'Have you really got a glider?'

'Will you take us up in it?'

'Please!'

There was no more teasing that day. But Michael and Richard and Edward didn't forget. All the year, they roared with laughter if anyone mentioned angels. And when they were on the way to Grandmother's again, next Christmas, Michael pointed up at the sky.

'Hey, Gabe! After the carol service — when I've sung the solo — we might go up in Mr King's glider.'

'*Really?*' Gabriel's eyes glittered, and he bounced up and down in his seat. 'Me too?'

'Why don't you ask?' Michael said solemnly. 'Look, we're just going past the garage.'

Gabriel was so excited that he stuck his head out of the window. 'Mr King! Can *I* go in your glider?'

'What's that?' Mr King came forward, out of his little glass cabin. 'Say it again, lad.'

But Michael didn't give him a chance. He stuck his head out too. 'Gabriel wants a ride in your glider. He thinks he'll turn into an angel.'

Mr King didn't laugh, but Gabriel realized that it was just a tease. He went pink and pulled his head back into the car.

The next day, Michael sang the solo at the carol service, and all the old ladies muttered about what an angel he was. Gabriel shrank down into the pew. It felt just as if they were laughing at him.

That was Michael's last year as an angel. In June, his voice broke, and he couldn't do anything except growl and croak. When Christmas came, it was Richard who sang the solo. And two years after that, Edward had to take over.

It was a tradition in Grandmother's village. The first verse of the first carol had always been sung as a solo, by a child.

O come, all ye faithful,
Joyful and triumphant,
O come ye, O come ye
To Bethlehem . . .

But there were no children in the choir any more — hardly any children in the village, in fact. So, every year, one of Gabriel's brothers sang instead, with his fair hair gleaming and his blue eyes bright. And all the old men in the congregation smiled, and the old women dabbed at their eyes.

And Gabriel sat there wondering how Michael (or Richard or Edward) could be so brave. Singing in front of all those people.

Then, when Gabriel was eight, Edward's voice broke. One day, just before Christmas, he came down to breakfast and started singing, and everyone burst out laughing.

Gabriel laughed too – but not for long. Because Edward grinned at him.

'Looks like you'll be singing the solo this Christmas.'

'*Me?*' It came out in a strangled squeak.

'You!' Michael and Richard and Edward yelled. And they laughed even more. They thought he was fussing about nothing.

'It's easy,' Michael said. 'You just need a bit of practice.'

They stood Gabriel on a chair and Richard started humming, pretending to be the organ. 'Come on, now. Sing. *O come all ye faithful* . . .'

Gabriel tried. But the more he tried, the less noise he could make. When he looked round at the three of them, all staring, he felt as if he were choking to death. The only sound that would come out of his mouth was a strangled squeak.

'*O cme all ye fthfl* . . .'

The others burst out laughing and he jumped off the chair and ran upstairs. And after that, when anyone suggested practising, he looked away and mumbled that he'd done enough practising.

'Dne nff pracsing.'

Everyone believed him. And they were sure he would be all right. Why shouldn't he be? Singing was easy. Nobody knew how scared he was.

The nearer they got to Christmas, the worse it grew.

When they were actually in the car, on the way to Grand-mother's, he was so scared that he thought he was going to faint. He couldn't smile, even though his brothers tried all the old jokes.

'Look, Gabe. Angels up in the sky!'

'Mr King's going to give us a ride in one of those gliders.'

'After you've sung your solo.'

Gabriel turned away and stared out of the window. He knew he was running out of time. When they arrived at Grandmother's, he had to go straight to bed. And the next day it was the carol service.

The moment he opened his eyes, he thought, *I've got to practise. Before it's too late.* Maybe he would be all right if he found a place where no one could hear him.

He walked down to the far end of the garden and hid behind a rhododendron bush. But the moment he opened his mouth, he began to worry that someone would come. And he made the same strangled sounds as before. *O cme all ye fthful . . .*

He tried locking himself in the bathroom and turning on all the taps. But was the noise really loud enough to drown out his voice? Before he could make up his mind, Grandmother banged on the door to ask him why he was wasting all that water.

He tried putting his head under the bedclothes, with all the pillows heaped on top. But that just made him suffocate, so that he gasped and panted. *O-ho c-h-me all ye f-h-thf-h-l . . .*

And then it was lunchtime. And he'd just picked up his knife and fork when Grandmother said, 'All ready for the rehearsal then, Gabriel?'

'Rehearsal?' Gabriel stared.

Michael grinned. 'Gabriel doesn't need a rehearsal.'

'Nonsense!' Grandmother said briskly. 'You all went to the rehearsal. That's why you sang so well. Gabriel must rehearse too. I'll take him down to church as soon as we've washed up.'

Gabriel had forgotten about the rehearsal. He'd hardly noticed last year, when Edward slipped off to church in the afternoon. But he remembered now, and he knew he couldn't do it.

He couldn't walk into the church with Grandmother, and stand in front of all those men and women in the choir and sing *O cme all ye fthfl* . . . He couldn't.

He would have to run away.

He didn't manage to eat much lunch, but everyone just smiled and said he was excited. Then they all went off to the kitchen to wash up in Double Quick Time. Grandmother liked everything done in Double Quick Time. Gabriel waited until they were laughing and talking and teasing each other. Then he opened the front door and slipped out.

There were only two ways to go – left and right. The road to the left went up to the church, so he turned the other way, automatically. He went downhill, towards the garage, running as fast as he could, to get out of sight before anyone saw him.

He ran too fast. As he passed the garage, he caught his foot on a loose stone and went tumbling over, scraping his knees along the ground and banging his head on the Tarmac.

For a moment he just lay there, thinking that things were as bad as they could possibly be. Then he remembered that they would be even worse if anyone caught him, because he'd have to go to the rehearsal. He groaned and started dragging himself up.

But he was too late. Mr King had seen him fall over. He came out of the little glass office behind the petrol pumps and inspected Gabriel's knees.

'Nasty fall,' he said calmly. 'Come in and have a barley sugar.'

For a moment, Gabriel thought of running away. Then he realized that Mr King might run after him. He followed him into the glass cabin, limping a bit.

Mr King unhooked a bag of barley sugars from the display, opened it and gave one to Gabriel. Then he said, 'What are you doing down here this afternoon? I thought you'd be up at the church. Rehearsing.'

That was the last straw. Before he could stop himself, Gabriel burst into tears.

Mr King pulled a handkerchief out of his pocket and unfolded it. He watched Gabriel wipe his eyes and then said, 'What's up?'

'Gt t sng n the crl svice,' mumbled Gabriel, with his face in his hands. 'Nd m scared –'

'No use talking like that,' Mr King said. 'You know I can't hear. Take your hands away from your mouth and let me lip-read.'

Gabriel had forgotten Mr King was deaf. Dropping his hands, he made himself speak clearly. He was concentrating so hard on making the shapes of the words with his lips, that he didn't worry about what he was saying.

'I've got to sing the solo at the carol service. And I'm scared.'

Mr King nodded. 'Not surprised. There's only one way to get over that. Practice.'

Gabriel hung his head. 'Bt –' Then he remembered about Mr King's deafness, and he started again. 'But if I practise, the others laugh at me.'

'So you can't sing? In case they laugh?'

Gabriel nodded.

Mr King gave him another barley sugar and walked up and down for a bit. Then he stopped and looked at Gabriel.

'Want to come up in a glider?'

'Me?' Gabriel was so amazed that he didn't mumble at all. Mr King had never offered any of the others a flight. Even though they'd begged him, for years and years. 'Just me?'

'Just you,' Mr King said. 'Come on.'

They walked out of the cabin and he locked it behind them. Then he turned the big sign at the front of the forecourt, so that it said CLOSED instead of OPEN.

'We've just got time before it's too dark. If we hurry.'

They climbed into his Land Rover and it started with a judder and bounced down the hill towards Mr King's house. When they got there, Mr King put on the brake, very noisily, and said something.

Gabriel couldn't hear at first, because of the engine. Then he remembered about lip-reading and he saw what Mr King was saying. *Wait there while I fetch my brothers.*

There were two brothers. They both had beards, but one was fat and one was thin. They smiled as they climbed into the back of the Land Rover. With a crash of gears, Mr King drove out of the village and up to the glider field.

Gabriel had been to the field dozens of times. Whenever they came to the village, his brothers walked up there and stared longingly at the hangar where Mr King kept his red and white glider. If he was there, Mr King would smile and wave to them, but he never asked them into the field.

This time, he drove straight in and round the track at the edge of the field.

'Stay in the Land Rover,' he said to Gabriel.

Gabriel knew what was going to happen, because he'd seen it before. He watched Mr King's brothers open the hangar and wheel out the glider. He watched Mr King prepare the winch, and unwind the long cable that would pull the glider into the air.

The brothers settled the glider at the far end of the field and left it there, with the sun gleaming on its red and white paint. Then they came back up to the hangar. The fat brother found a helmet.

'Scared?' he said, as he adjusted the straps round Gabriel's chin.

'No.' Gabriel didn't see how anyone could be scared about going up in a glider. How could you be afraid of something wonderful?

Climbing into the cockpit, he settled himself in the front seat, with Mr King behind him. His heart was thudding against his ribs, but he knew he wasn't scared. He was excited.

The thin brother held on to the glider's wing and the fat one went down the field, to start the winch. Suddenly, the glider was racing forward, pulled by the cable. The thin brother ran along beside, holding it level.

'Here we go!' said Mr King.

And the glider took off.

It went up like a bird. Like an arrow shot from a bow. Rising into the air like something speeding up a steep, steep hill. Gabriel felt himself being pushed against the back of his seat. Up and up and up . . .

And then they stopped climbing.

'Look over the side,' Mr King's voice said, from behind.

Gabriel turned his head and saw the winch cable falling away as the glider levelled out. The cable had done its work and pulled them up, just as the string pulls a kite. Now they were in the sky, floating free. Riding the currents of the air.

It was very quiet. The only sounds Gabriel could hear were the creak of the wooden wings and the hiss of air round his head. He was sitting high in the sky, with nothing to shut him in.

Far below, he could see the village. The church where the choir was singing. The cars racing round the bypass. A train in the distance. They were all too far away to hear.

For a few minutes, the glider circled slowly, and Gabriel stared round. He was amazed how clearly he could see everything, even though it was such a long way down. It was like looking at the whole world.

'Beautiful, isn't it?' Mr King said.

Gabriel nodded. There was no way of saying how beautiful it was.

Mr King gave a small, soft chuckle. 'Always makes me want to sing.'

'*Do* you sing?' Gabriel said. 'Up here on your own?'

There was another chuckle. 'No use talking. I can't lip-read from here. Can't hear a thing you're saying.'

For a second, Gabriel felt stupid.

And then he understood what Mr King was telling him. They were up there on their own, just the two of them. And Mr King was deaf. *So no one could possibly hear any singing. No one in the whole world!*

But – wasn't it ridiculous? Singing in a glider?

Gabriel looked over the side, at the grey church spire, and the glittering line of the brook, and the big hills stretching away into the distance. The lovely, sunlit world. No, singing wasn't ridiculous. It was the only sensible thing to do.

He opened his mouth.

O come all ye faithful,
Joyful and triumphant . . .

It felt wonderful. Like yelling hurrah. Like blowing a fanfare on a trumpet.

Like being an angel.

The white wings of the glider gleamed in the winter sunshine. There was a small green car driving round the bypass. Maybe there was a little boy inside. Looking up at the glider and thinking it was an angel. Gabriel took a deep breath and sang as loudly and sweetly as he could.

O come let us adore him,
O come let us adore him,
O come let us adore him,
Christ the Lord!

He was still singing as the glider circled lower over the field. He didn't even realize they were landing, until they bumped lightly on to the grass, and Mr King's brothers came running forward to help him out of his seat.

'That was a nice bit of singing,' said the thin brother.

'Look forward to hearing you in church,' said the fat brother.

Gabriel went pink and hung his head. 'Bt tht's diffrnt.'

Mr King tapped his shoulder. 'What did you say?'

Gabriel felt silly, but he turned round and spoke clearly. 'I said that's different. Singing in church.'

'Don't see why,' Mr King said. 'Shut your eyes, and you can be anywhere you like.'

The brothers both nodded, and Gabriel frowned. What did they mean?

'Time to go home,' Mr King said. 'I'll take you up. These two will put the glider away. Hop in the Land Rover, lad.'

As Gabriel climbed in, he suddenly wondered what he was going to say when he got back to Grandmother's house. She would be furious with him. How could he explain why he'd run away?

He didn't have to explain anything. When they reached the house, Mr King went in on his own, leaving Gabriel to wait in the Land Rover. When he came out again, Grandmother was with him. She was smiling.

'You've missed the rehearsal, but it sounds as though you don't need one. Mr King tells me you're a wonderful singer.'

'But —' *But Mr King can't hear . . .*

Grandmother didn't give Gabriel time to say it. She caught hold of his arm. 'Hurry up, or we'll be late for the service.'

Michael came bounding out of the house in his best clothes. 'Gabriel can't go to church like that. He's wearing jeans.'

'Don't be silly,' Grandmother said. 'And anyway, no one will see when he's got the choir robes on. Come along, Gabriel.'

She hustled him down the path, with the rest of the family scurrying behind. Michael ran to catch up, whispering in Gabriel's ear.

'Where have you been?'

'In a glider,' Gabriel said.

'Oh, ha ha!' Michael pulled a face. 'Stop teasing.'

Teasing? 'Mr King took me up.'

Richard jogged up. 'Don't be silly. The garage is open on Friday afternoons. Mr King must have been there.'

Gabriel couldn't answer, because they'd reached the church, and Grandmother was chivvying him round to the vestry. She buttoned him into a long blue cassock and slipped a white surplice over his head. Then she nodded approvingly.

'You look very nice. Even better than your brothers.'

Gabriel didn't care how he looked. As she pushed him into line with the rest of the choir, he was shaking. And when they walked into church, he nearly fainted. All the front pews were full. People were going to *hear* him. He couldn't sing. He *couldn't*.

The organist began the introduction to the first carol. Gabriel felt his throat go dry. He knew he wouldn't be able to make any sound except a squeak. He knew it. But there was no escape.

He opened his mouth.

And then, at the last moment, he saw Mr King, sitting at the back of the church, looking at him. Slowly and deliberately, Mr King closed his eyes. *Shut your eyes, and you can be anywhere you like.*

All at once, Gabriel understood. He closed his own eyes – and he wasn't looking at rows of people any more. He was in the glider, circling like an angel. The sunshine was glittering on the snow-white wings, and the beautiful world was spread out below.

He started to sing, as sweetly as he could.

O come all ye faithful . . .

He didn't open his eyes until the whole carol was over. When he did, he saw his brothers, sitting in the front pew, staring at him. Wondering whether it could be possibly true about the glider. He almost burst out laughing.

But he didn't laugh. He stared straight ahead, looking solemn and good, and he heard the old ladies whispering to each other.

'Just like an angel . . .'

I'll do it even better next year, he thought. And he started smiling. He had years and years left before his voice broke. Years and years of being a Christmas angel.

The Real Father Christmas

KATE PETTY

'Well, Father Christmas is bringing me a watch,' said large Lucy, her thick hair bouncing and her arm firmly tucked in Nicky Barlow's as they trooped up the stairs after Assembly. 'And clothes. And I always get some CDs and books and stuff ... and the usual stocking-y things of course. God, I love Christmas, don't you?' Large Lucy beamed down at her diminutive friend.

At times like this, Nicky was glad she wore glasses. They made her feelings less transparent.

They wheeled into the classroom. 'Don't you just love Christmas, miss?' Lucy asked Miss Cole, their teacher.

'Oh yes, I love Christmas,' said Miss Cole. She gave a warm smile to large Lucy's anxious friend and the thought crossed her mind that Nicky might not have so much to look forward to this Christmas. 'But right now we've got some tables to learn. Tomorrow, however, we're going to find out about the *real* Father Christmas, so save all your talk until then.'

Jan Barlow was up when Nicky let herself in. Nicky hugged her, shocked as always by the way her cuddly mum had turned bony.

'Do you want some tea with me now, or do you want to wait until the boys get in?' Mum asked.

'With you, Mum. You might be resting when they get in.' Nicky's mum didn't have much energy, because of the way her cancer was at the moment, but she made it her business to cook the family meal, even if it took all day and she was too tired to eat with them.

'Go and flop in a chair then. The kettle's boiled.'

Nicky humoured her mum and climbed into the big armchair by the gas fire.

'They're all on about Christmas at school – you know, what presents they're going to get,' Nicky said. Mum liked to hear about her day. Inside her head Nicky was thinking, They'd never understand what I really want for Christmas, far, far more than any present. But she didn't need to say the actual words. Mum understood. She came over with the big old teapot and two cups.

'And all you want is a well mother? I know, sweetheart. But *I* intend to have a great Christmas. For once I've got the time to think about what to give you all, and lots of willing helpers to go shopping for me. So you'd better start thinking about what *you* want from Father Christmas!'

Fat lot of use he is, Nicky thought grimly.

Miss Cole quelled the hubbub in the classroom. Lucy was actually on a chair shouting, 'Well, he's bringing me a watch,' at Dominic who was countering with, 'So! He's bringing me a new computer!' and Justin who said, 'And he's bringing me the really expensive trainers –'

'What a materialistic little bunch we have here!' said Miss Cole. 'Have you all completely forgotten that Christmas is about giving, not getting? Now sit down all of you, and let's talk about the real Santa Claus and what he means to us now.'

Miss Cole told her class about St Nicholas (perhaps he was Nicky for short, too, Nicky thought). 'Nicholas was a bishop who lived in a place called Myra – which is now in Turkey – sixteen hundred years ago. Nicholas always loved children, so when he died he became their patron saint. In Germany and Holland people used to dress up as bishops on his special day – December 6th –

and give presents to good children in his memory. And in their language St Nicholas became Santa Claus! It wasn't until the last century that this custom spread to other parts of the world. Now we picture him as a jolly old man dressed in red. He still only gives presents to good children though, on Christmas Eve these days. Some children get him muddled up with their ideas of God – another old-man figure who knows if they're being god or bad!'

'Does that mean he *is* real then, miss?' asked Dominic.

'I don't know,' said Miss Cole carefully. 'Let's ask around the class and see what other people think, shall we?'

'We don't have Father Christmas, miss,' said Rajiv, laughing. 'We don't have Christmas!'

'We don't have them either,' said Rebekah. 'Jews have Hannukah instead. But we do have food, and candles – and presents.'

'Fancy not having a stocking!' said Lucy, horrified. 'Actually, I get a pillowcase. And it's stuffed full of big presents! Did you have a stocking, miss? In the olden days, when you were a little girl?'

'I did,' said Miss Cole. 'It was full of inexpensive, tiny things though. And there was always a balloon to blow up and a tangerine at the bottom. I used to think I could hear the sleigh bells, when I was little, from Father Christmas's reindeer. My big brothers and sisters always told me I could. Now, what about you, Lucy? What are your thoughts on Father Christmas?

'Kids' stuff!' said Lucy. 'But he *does* bring me presents.'

'I stopped believing in him years ago!' said Justin. 'But *someone* fills my stocking when I hang it up!'

Miss Cole had come to Won Kah-ho. 'What about you, Kah-ho?'

'We don't have Christmas, miss. Well, we sort of do when we're in England. I went and saw Father Christmas in the department store once — but I don't think he was the real one . . .'

Miss Cole had come to Nicky. 'What about you, Nicky?'

'No,' said Nicky. 'No, I don't believe in Father Christmas.'

Jan Barlow's Christmas list was long. Nicky and her older brother Paul set out early the Saturday before Christmas to do her shopping. Nicky looked at the list. It was as if Mum had really enjoyed choosing what to give people. Every present was different. Every one suited the person it was for. Nicky could just see Mum imagining their happy faces as they received them.

The high street was bright and Christmassy. The Salvation-Army band was playing outside Boots. A bunch of little kids was singing carols at the other end. The air was cold and crisp. Dads carried Christmas trees; families laughed together.

'I'm really looking forward to this now, Nicks,' said Paul. 'Let's work our way down from the top end of the high street first, then I'll buy us something to eat. We'll do the other end after that and then I'll help you buy Mum's present. OK?'

OK,' said Nicky, and was soon caught up in the cheerful crowds.

They were laden with carrier bags when they emerged from the coffee shop to start on their second stint. Nicky had seen a beautiful tiny teapot and a selection of herb teas to give Mum and she was going back to buy them when they were finished.

She spotted him first just outside Marks and Spencers. He was a big man with a full head of white hair and a beard. He wore a sort of brown knitted hat on his head and his sludge-coloured coat was held together round the middle with string. He shuffled down the street ahead of them to the sleeping bag and beer cans that marked out his pitch. There was a radio there too. But there was no mistaking who he was. Nicky gasped. She tugged at her brother's sleeve. 'Paul, look!'

'What at?' Paul couldn't see anything unusual.

'That man!'

'What about him? He's out of his head, but he won't hurt you, don't worry.'

Nicky decided not to say anything, but she knew that she had just seen Father Christmas.

It took another two hours to buy everything on Mum's list. They were exhausted, but Nicky still wanted to go back for Mum's little teapot. 'Why don't I wait here with the bags,' said Paul as they came to some benches by the carol singers. 'You can find your own way, can't you? There's M & S and it's the shop next door. Be grown-up. Just don't talk to any strange men, OK? I won't move from here.'

Nicky set off for Marks and Spencers, her purse a pleasant weight in her pocket. She'd been collecting small change for ages and she knew she had just enough for Mum's present. It was nice being on her own. She was looking forward to buying the teapot and even more to seeing Mum's face when she opened it. But between her and the teapot shop was – Father Christmas. His radio was playing and he was waving about in front of his sleeping bag with his arms in the air and a can of beer in his hand, doing a sort of shambling dance. He kept stumbling and swearing. Nicky could see that he was quite pathetic, but she watched him, mesmerised. He sang a slurred little song along with the radio as he stepped from side to side. Tears sprang to Nicky's eyes. Here was an old man, old enough to be a grandad. Why was he out on the streets at Christmas? Why wasn't he in the pub having a cheerful pint with the other old gaffers? What had happened? What had gone so horribly wrong in his life?

'Spare us some change?' he was leering, close. He must have seen her watching. 'Enjoying the entertainment, love? Put on a good show, don't I?' Nicky backed away. He smelt very strong. He carried on his terrible tap dancing.

Nicky didn't know what to do. She wanted to magic him into a clean and jolly old man with a wave of a wand. She had thought he was Father Christmas, for heaven's sake. But worse, deep down, below the sophisticated layers of an older Nicky, a part of her believed even now that he was Father Christmas. Father Christmas, who made so many children happy, had come to this. But there was nothing she could do. Well, there was something.

On an impulse, Nicky dug into her purse in her pocket. She brought out a handful of coins and tossed them on to the sleeping bag before running blindly on and into the doors of the teapot shop.

Nicky gathered up the little teapot and two mixed boxes of herb teabags. There was rosehip and hibiscus to help Mum wake up in the morning, chamomile to help her sleep, mint to refresh her and lemon and ginger to pep her up. Nicky knew she'd love them. She put the pot and the boxes on the counter and dug out her purse. 'That will be seven pounds and eighty-eight pence, please,' said the girl on the till, starting to wrap the teapot in tissue paper. Nicky pulled out the eighty-eight pence, then two pound coins, and another two . . . That was it. Her purse was empty. She had given Father Christmas the money she'd saved for Mum!

'Is anything the matter?' All the colour had drained from Nicky's face.

'Could I just have the teabags, please?' said Nicky weakly.

'Sure,' said the girl in a bored way. 'That'll be two pounds and thirty-eight pence, please.'

Nicky ran back to Paul and told him what had happened.

'Silly old Nicks,' he said. 'He'll only spend it on booze.'

'But I wanted him to have a nice Christmas,' said Nicky. She didn't dare tell her brother that she'd thought the tramp was Father Christmas.

Dad said much the same thing when Nicky told him, but he also saw that the generous spirit of his wife was alive and well in his daughter, so he put his arm around her. 'Perhaps he won't buy booze this time. Perhaps he'll buy himself a nice pair of warm gloves or socks or a hot meal. After all, he saw that a warm-hearted little girl gave him all that money.'

In the safety of her father's arms, Nicky felt she could tell him, 'The thing was, Dad, he looked just like Father Christmas. Really. And I thought of all the presents that Father Christmas had given to children, year after year after year, and that he ought to have one himself for a change.'

Dad hugged her tighter. 'Come with me now, Nicky. There's still time to buy the teapot before the shop shuts. I'll advance you some of January's pocket money. Perhaps I'll be lucky enough to catch a glimpse of this Father Christmas of yours, too!'

Nicky and Dad went out again. The High Street was quieter, but a new group of musicians were playing carols by the Christmas tree and coloured lights made everywhere magical. 'I still love Christmas,' Nicky told Dad. 'Let's drive Mum down here when we get back so that she can see it all too.'

'Good idea,' said Dad. 'We can't pretend Mum isn't ill, Nicks, but she's more alive than most people I know. And she'll be like that for a long time yet, maybe longer than we think. We must remember that.'

Nicky and Dad bought the little teapot. They came out of the shop and past Marks and Spencers. But the tramp had vanished. There was no sign of him. No sleeping bag. No radio.

'He's gone!' Nicky began to wonder if she'd imagined him. 'But he was there, Dad, honestly.'

'Oh, I believe you,' said Dad. He smiled at his wide-eyed daughter. 'But I'm not surprised he's gone. He obviously had an important job to do.'

'Exactly,' said Nicky, and squeezed Dad's hand as they walked past all the lit-up Christmas trees in the windows, home to Mum.

Why the Chimes Rang

RAYMOND MacDONALD ALDEN

There was once, in a faraway country where few people have ever travelled, a wonderful church. It stood on a high hill in the midst of a great city; and every Sunday, as well as on sacred days like Christmas, thousands of people climbed the hill to its great archways, looking like lines of ants all moving in the same direction.

When you came to the building itself, you found stone columns and dark passages, and a grand entrance leading to a main room of the church. This room was so long that one standing at the doorway could scarcely see to the other end, where the choir stood by the marble altar. In the farthest corner was the organ; and this organ was so loud that, sometimes when it played, the people for miles around would close their shutters and prepare for a great thunderstorm. Altogether, no such church as this was ever seen before, especially when it was lighted up for some festival, and crowded with people, young and old. But the strangest thing about the whole building was the wonderful chime of bells.

At one corner of the church was a great grey tower, with ivy growing over it as far up as one could see. I say as far as one could see, because the tower was quite great enough to fit the great church, and it rose so far into the sky that it was only in very fair weather that anyone claimed to be able to see the top.

Even then one could not be certain that it was in sight. Up, and up, and up climbed the stones and the ivy; and, as the men who built the church had been dead for hundreds of years, everyone had forgotten how high the tower was supposed to be.

Now all the people knew that at the top of the tower was a chime of Christmas bells. They had hung there ever since the church had been built, and were the most beautiful bells in the world. Some thought it was because a great musician had cast them and arranged them in their place; others said it was because of the great height, which reached up where the air was clearest and purest; however that might be, no one who had ever heard the chimes denied that they were the sweetest in the world. Some described them as sounding like angels far up in the sky; others, as sounding like strange winds singing throughout the trees.

But the fact was that no one had heard them for years and years. There was an old man living not far from the church, who said that his mother had spoken of hearing them when she was a little girl, and he was the only one who was sure of as much as that. They were Christmas chimes, you see, and were not meant to be played by men or on common days. It was the custom on Christmas Eve for all the people to bring to the church their offerings to the Christ Child; and when the greatest and best offering was laid on the altar, there used to come sounding through the music of the choir the Christmas chimes far up in the tower. Some said that the wind rang them, and others that they were so high that the angels could set them swinging. But for many long years they had never been heard. It was said that people had been growing less careful of their gifts for the Christ Child, and that no offering was brought, great enough to deserve the music of the chimes.

Every Christmas Eve the rich people still crowded to the altar, each one trying to bring some better gift than any other, without giving anything that he wanted for himself, and the church was crowded with those who thought that perhaps the wonderful bells might be heard again. But although the service was splendid, and the offerings plenty, only the roar of the wind could be heard, far up in the stone tower.

Now, a number of miles from the city, in a little country village, where nothing could be seen of the great church but glimpses of the tower when the weather was fine, lived a boy named Pedro, and his little brother. They knew very little about the Christmas chimes, but they had heard of the service in the church on Christmas Eve, and had a secret plan, which they had often talked over when by themselves, to go to see the beautiful celebration.

'Nobody can guess, Little Brother,' Pedro would say, 'all the fine things there are to see and hear; and I have even heard it said that the Christ Child sometimes comes down to bless the service. What if we could see Him?'

The day before Christmas was bitterly cold, with a few lonely snowflakes flying in the air, and a hard white crust on the ground. Sure enough, Pedro and Little Brother were able to slip quietly away early in the afternoon; and although the walking was hard in the frosty air, before nightfall they had trudged so far, hand in hand, that they saw the lights of the big city just ahead of them. Indeed, they were about to enter one of the great gates in the wall that surrounded it, when they saw something dark on the snow near their path, and stepped aside to look at it.

It was a poor woman, who had fallen just outside the city, too sick and tired to get in where she might have found shelter. The soft snow made of a drift a sort of pillow for her, and she would soon be so sound asleep, in the wintry air, that no one could ever waken her again.

All this Pedro saw in a moment, and he knelt down beside her and tried to rouse her, even tugging at her arm a little, as though he would have tried to carry her away. He turned her face towards him, so that he could rub some of the snow on it, and when he had looked at her silently a moment he stood up again, and said:

'It's no use, Little Brother. You will have to go on alone.'

'Alone?' cried Little Brother. 'And you not see the Christmas festival?'

'No,' said Pedro, and he could not keep back a bit of a choking sound in his throat. 'See this poor woman. Her face looks like the Madonna in the chapel window, and she will freeze to death if nobody cares for her. Everyone has gone to the church now, but when you come back you can bring someone to help her. I will rub her to keep her from freezing, and perhaps get her to eat the bun that is left in my pocket.'

'But I cannot bear to leave you, and go on alone,' said Little Brother.

'Both of us need not miss the service,' said Pedro, 'and

it had better be I than you. You can easily find your way to the church; and you must see and hear everything twice, Little Brother — once for you and once for me. I am sure the Christ Child must know how I should love to come with you and worship Him; and oh! if you get a chance, Little Brother, to slip up to the altar without getting in anyone's way, take this little silver piece of mine, and lay it down for my offering, when no one is looking. Do not forget where you have left me, and forgive me for not going with you.'

In this way he hurried Little Brother off to the city, and winked hard to keep back the tears, as he heard the crunching footsteps sounding farther and farther away in the twilight. It was pretty hard to lose the music and splendour of the Christmas celebration that he had been planning for so long, and spend the time instead in that lonely place in the snow.

The great church was a wonderful place that night. Everyone said that it had never looked so bright and beautiful before. When the organ played and the thousands of people sang, the walls shook with the sound, and little Pedro, away outside the city wall, felt the earth tremble around him.

At the close of the service came the procession with the offerings to be laid on the altar. Rich men and great men marched proudly up to lay down their gifts to the

Christ Child. Some brought wonderful jewels, some baskets of gold so heavy that they could scarcely carry them down the aisle. A great writer laid down a book that he had been making for years and years. And last of all walked the king of the country, hoping with all the rest to win for himself the chime of the Christmas bells. There went a great murmur throughout the church, as the people saw the king take from his head the royal crown, all set with precious stones, and lay it gleaming on the altar, as his offering to the Holy Child. 'Surely,' everyone said, 'we shall hear the bells now, for nothing like this has ever happened before.'

But still only the cold old wind was heard in the tower, and the people shook their heads; and some of them said, as they had before, that they never really believed the story of the chimes, and doubted if they ever rang at all.

The procession was over, and the choir began the closing hymn. Suddenly the organist stopped playing as though he had been shot, and everyone looked at the old minister, who was standing by the altar, holding up his hand for silence. Not a sound could be heard from anyone in the church, but as all the people strained their ears to listen, there came softly, but distinctly, swinging through the air, the sound of the chimes in the tower. So far away, and yet so clear the music seemed – so much sweeter were the notes than anything that had been heard before, rising and falling away up there in the sky, that the people in the church sat for a moment as still as though something held each of them by the shoulders. Then they all stood up together and stared straight at the altar, to see what great gift had awakened the long-silent bells.

But all that the nearest of them saw was the childish figure of Little Brother, who had crept softly down the aisle when no one was looking, and had laid Pedro's little piece of silver on the altar.

Little Brown Jesus

JOAN O'DONOVAN

'Pause,' I said again. 'You forgot the pause.'

The Virgin Mary's eyes rolled in her brown-sugar face.

'Yes, Miss,' she said resignedly.

'Try once more. And watch me.'

'*Pause!*' I said.

This time, Heliotrope bared her teeth in a wide, semi-circular grin.

'You do have to keep saying it!' she told me with enthusiasm.

I gave up. It was the fifteenth time that morning.

'All right, that'll do for now.'

They were round me then, the children, twittering. This was the backward class, only at Gudge Street we called it 'Opportunity'. Gabrielle had torn his halo and the fifth shepherd had lost his lines.

'You must remember to watch the beat,' I said to Heliotrope as I put a stitch in the halo. 'I'm not standing up there to scare the birds.'

Heliotrope jigged happily and her pencil-pigtails, each harvested from a square of black wool and tied with red tape, stood on end . . . all eight of them.

'In Jamaica we got things like a drain, miss, with holes; and the boys cover them with grass so the birds don't see, and when they stand there they catch their legs and the boys put them in cages.'

She giggled and flattened her nose with a gesture of splayed fingers.

'Crool thing!' shouted Jim.

The class took it up.

'I'n't that Heliotrope crool, Miss?'

'That Heliotrope' was her usual designation.

It wasn't that the children didn't like her. You couldn't dislike her any more you could dislike a puppy. But, with one exception, they preferred to keep their distance; for Heliotrope wasn't just naughty, she was dynamite. Even Jim, who had in his time thrown a bucket of worms at the needlework mistress and hit the caretaker with his own broom, tried to protect himself when she was around by sidling up to me and mumbling superstitiously. 'T'n'it awful, Miss, when there's *trouble*?'

I knew what he meant. Anything might happen. There had never been a colour problem at Gudge Street before Heliotrope came, but she had started one on her first day by calling us dirty whites. She was nearly lynched.

Oddly enough, it was Doreen Bax, the quietest girl in the class, who had become Heliotrope's friend; and now, it seemed, the play was going to put paid to that, for ... it was most unfortunate ... Doreen had assumed she would be the Virgin. She was a pale, pretty girl with an oval face, soft curling hair and wide blue eyes. And she always had been the Virgin. When a doubt arose, her mother sent me a sharp note, with cuttings from the local paper and a tinted photograph. That settled it. I'm obstinate too. In my play she was an angel. She had been sulking for a fortnight.

The morning of the dress rehearsal came ... we were to act the play for the school in the afternoon ... and, to kick off, Gertie Pugh stole the blob of red glass from the tea cosy worn by the first wise man under the impression that it was what she called a *jool*. We managed to coax it from her knicker leg, but it took time; and as, in snatching it, she had broken the pin, I had to stick it back on the tea cosy with glue. Then Jim (seventh shepherd) had a fit of nerves and knocked Joseph down; and the innkeeper's wife turned up with a yellow crinoline, long black gloves and a Dolly Varden hat, which her mother's interpretation of my request for an old sheet and a couple of safety pins; and she unnerved me further by going out to assembly in the hat and gloves. But worse than all that, far worse, was the crisis over the doll.

I had suggested that a bundle wrapped in a shawl was all that was needed for a stage baby, but the class wasn't having any. Even Jim, who sucked up to me in his calm spells, couldn't bring himself to let that pass.

'Anyone'd see it wasn't Jesus in them clothes,' he explained. 'Up our church they had a doll, miss. And strore.'

Jim was an overgrown, loose-meshed boy with poor co-ordination and thick hobnails. Sometimes he fell flat on his face. It was news to me that he ever went to church.

'Yes, Miss!' The class was censorious. 'You gotter have a doll!'

So I chose Doreen to bring hers. It seemed to cheer her up.

'And strore,' Jim reminded me. 'It i'n't right without strore.'

'All right, Jim, if you can get any straw, you bring it.'

But I wasn't sorry when he turned up without it, for I had troubles enough. Certainly, Doreen brought her doll, a little cuddly doll – a black doll. But Heliotrope brought a doll too, a white doll; and Heliotrope's doll was three foot tall and very much a lady doll.

'I got Jesus, miss!' she said.

The class gazed rapt at the sequined ball dress and stiletto heels.

'It's bigger'n the one I seen up church,' Jim gloated. 'T'n'it like a film star?'

He was right on both counts.

Doreen clutched her doll to her, and her face went slowly scarlet. Foolishly, I tried persuasion.

'That's a beautiful doll, Heliotrope, but I think it's a bit big.'

'Big, Miss?' Heliotrope went into a squeal of incredulous laughter. 'Bit? This nothing! Why . . .'

'Besides,' I interrupted, 'Doreen has brought hers. I asked her to, you know. It was all arranged.'

Heliotrope affected astonishment.

'Do you mean that little doll?' Her voice was objective. 'That small one? I don't think that's good enough to be Jesus, Miss, that *little* doll.'

I had never before heard Doreen raise her voice. I should have said she was incapable of it. But it came now in a screech of rage.

'Jesus wasn't a *lady*!'

Heliotrope turned on her. The gloves were off.

'Jesus could've been anything he liked!' she snapped. 'He could've been a mouse, or a lion . . . anything! It says so in the Bible.'

'Well, he was a baby in the *play*, Heliotrope Smith, so there!'

I expected the class to concede that, but, hypnotized, the children continued to stare at the film star and Heliotrope made the most of it. She narrowed her cat-eyes to dull, spiteful slits.

'Your doll's black!' she said baldly. 'The one thing Jesus never was was black. Jesus was real white.' She jutted a shoulder contemptuously. 'Little black thing!'

'Babies *are* little! We got one.'

'Little! Only bad, low-class babies are little! Why, I seen babies in Jamaica, *huge* babies! Their mammies could hardly lift them . . .'

'Babies are little,' Doreen repeated stubbornly. 'And my doll says "Ma-ma" like our baby does.'

Furious, she shook the coloured doll and it bleated.

'So does mine! So does mine!'

Heliotrope tipped her doll at a dangerous angle. It had a powerful voice, like a tenor bull . . .

Doreen began to cry.

'Mine walks too!' she sobbed.

Heliotrope cast a triumphant eye round the class.

'Mine walks . . .' she screamed '. . . *and* wets!' And

snatching up the ball dress, she revealed an incongruous pair of rubber pants.

It was time to stop the demonstrations. We would rehearse, I said firmly, with a bundle. The dolls were put aside and the decision shelved till the afternoon. With luck, one of the children might come out in a rash and have to be sent home.

At lunchtime, I took four more aspirins and went to lie down. The rest of the staff were in the canteen, so I had the staff-room to myself. The playground noises came filtered by the distance, rare and a little unearthly. I began to relax. The Head, after all, was a reasonable man. He wouldn't expect the Opportunity class to do more than lumber on and lumber off; and let's face it, I told myself, that's all they'll do. But did it matter? Whatever happened, the Opportunity class would be delighted. The Opportunity class had a great welcome for itself.

I was woken from a light doze by a pounding of boots on the stairs, and a terrible boy called Fisher burst in.

'You're wanted,' he told me.

He was wearing Edwardian dress, a long velvet drape and a tie no thicker than a shoelace. I had an impulse to ask him why he did it, but thought better of it.

'Who wants me?' I said instead. 'What is it?'

'A man wiv an 'orse and cart.'

It came to me like a symbol in a dream. I went downstairs, past the children swinging on the main door and out into the stale cold of Gudge Street. A woman walked by with a cabbage under her arm and a thick, worn purse in her thick, worn hand. Opposite, a youth lounged in a doorway eating chips from a bag. But there was no man that I could see, and no cart, no horse.

Kennick, on playground duty, wandered across.

'You owe me fifty pence.' He held out his hand. 'Walton couldn't find you. I sent Fisher, but the bloke wouldn't wait so I paid.'

'What for?'

'He said for obliging.'

I gave him the money and he looked at me curiously. 'Aren't you having fun!'

I didn't answer. I was thinking of my predecessors. One was still in hospital. I decided that I must be less sincere about my job. I must look after myself. I must keep a grip on reality; and next time I mustn't take so much aspirin.

But back in the classroom the nightmare met me, and it had nothing to do with mental balance. Straw. A mountain of straw. My desk was submerged, and the top of the radiator showed like the fluted edging of a flower bed. Spikes stuck at bizarre angles from the inkwells, and the air was thick with dust.

I stared stupidly round. I tried to wade forward, but

barked my shin against the nature table which I could no longer see. I was rescuing the terrapins when Jim skated up.

'I ain't letcher down!' he told me happily. 'My dad says it's all right about the strore. The fifty pence was for the rag-and-bone man that lent him the 'orse. There was too much to go on his barrer.' He tossed a handful joyously. 'It's more than we had up our church.'

'It was very generous of your dad, Jim,' I said in a controlled voice.

'Tha'sall right, Miss!' He threw another fistful up and it came down on me. He began to scratch. 'Fleas,' he said cheerfully. 'You don't half get a lotter fleas in strore.'

When Heliotrope came in I saw she had a long scratch on her cheek, and Doreen had the beginnings of a black eye. The class was exhausted. It must have been quite an emotional dinner hour.

But there was still fight in Heliotrope.

'Miss,' she demanded in the voice of one who will be trifled with no longer, 'which doll is Jesus?'

She didn't press her point, but I knew that look. If I wasn't careful, I could whistle for my Virgin.

Weakly, I glanced at Doreen. The swollen eye gave her an air of unwonted toughness, and for the first time I detected a resemblance to her mother. I felt I couldn't stand that either; so I asked myself the question that

I had the occasion to ask myself many times with the Opportunity class: What would King Solomon the wise have done now?

And then it came to me, the one solution possible.

'We're going to have two Jesuses,' I said crisply.

Now that's where I hand it to an Opportunity class. There's no conventional prejudice.

'Smashing!' shouted Jim. 'They only had one up our church!'

Heliotrope brightened. She began to giggle. Doreen's face lit into a slow, satisfied smile. They looked at each other. Heliotrope pranced up and flung an arm round her rival's neck.

'You know,' she said judicially, 'mebbe your little Jesus isn't so black as I thought. Mebbe he's just a little brown Jesus.'

She took him up and began to nurse him.

So the film star lay in the crib; or half of her did. The nylon legs and stiletto heels were embedded in the merciful strore.

And, really, it was astonishing, but no one forgot his words, not even Jim. True, the jool came unstuck and fell at Mary's feet, but I liked the symbolism; and, when it came to it, Doreen looked interesting in profile, and I alone could see the ripening eye. As for Heliotrope, she rooted the Christmas story in Gudge Street, and Gudge

Street paid her the tribute of absorbed silence. After all, these were the threatened children, the children of flits, evictions and eight to a room: they understood about having it the hard way.

I watched from the wings as the play swept through to its climax. There was just the solo now, and it would be over for another year. I raised a hand, the other on the pulley; and Heliotrope, alone on the stage, waited as I had told her to wait. The air was so still that I heard a man whistling a street away. But when we had both counted to ten, she looked, not at me but at the bundle in her arms; and instead of beginning 'Away in a Manger', she sang to a beat that I recognized as calypso:

'Little brown Jesus, go sleep um don't cry . . .'

I turned frightened eyes to the school. There was a sense of feet tapping, but not a foot moved: and Heliotrope, easing herself as a mother nursing a baby might, sang with a sort of loving exasperation:

Little brown Jesus, go sleep um don't cry;
When you cry so bad you make Mammy boil.
Your Daddy Joseph he gone saw wood,
And Lord God he is busy with the weather,
So you go sleep, you brown-skin boy,
Your Mammie done smack you when you don't go sleep . . .

The voice got quieter. Heliotrope cast me a single authoritative glance, and the glance said *Curtain!*

'Um Lord . . . U-u-um Lor-ord!'

I let the curtain slowly down.

Silence continued for perhaps five seconds; then thunder broke. I dashed on to the stage and caught Heliotrope up. She giggled wildly, and flung her arms and legs round me like a monkey.

'What you crying for, Miss?'

'Write it out! You must write it down for me, that song! Do you hear?'

I felt the heart go out of her.

'Yes, miss,' she said dully.

I remembered then. For Heliotrope, writing was a punishment and a pain.

'No, no, silly!' I said. 'I like your song. I want to have it! You tell me the words: I'll write them down myself!'

She threw herself back and squealed with laughter, her limbs twitching with diabolical energy again.

'Hoo! I thought you was cross!' She looked at me now as if she feared I was daft instead. 'I just sing to brown Jesus, see, Miss? Any old words. They just come.' She giggled again. 'I forgot to watch for you scaring them birds, didn't I?'

The Box of Magic

MALORIE BLACKMAN

It was Christmas Eve, but Peter was in no hurry. His head bent, Peter dragged his feet as he made his way slowly home. There was no point in rushing. Mum and Dad would only be arguing about something or another. Peter and his sister Chloe had hoped that the quarrelling would stop over Christmas. It hadn't. If anything, it'd got worse.

Peter had spent all afternoon searching and searching for the perfect present for his mum and dad. Something that would stop them quarrelling for just five minutes. Something that would make Christmas the way it used to be, with smiles and songs and happiness in every corner of the house. But all the searching had been for nothing. Peter didn't have that much money to begin with and all the things he could afford, he didn't want. All the gifts he could afford looked so cheap and tacky that Peter knew they would fall apart about ten seconds after they were handled. What was he going to do? He had to buy something and time was running out.

Then he caught sight of it out of the corner of his eye.

The medium-sized sign above the door said 'THE CHRISTMAS SHOP' in spidery writing. The small shop window was framed with silver and gold tinsel and a scattering of glitter like mini stars. At the bottom of the window, fake snow had been sprayed. It looked so much like the real thing that had it been outside the window instead of inside, Peter would've been sure it was real snow. A single Christmas tree, laden down with fairy lights and baubles and yet more tinsel, stood proudly in the exact centre of the window.

Peter stood in front of the shop and stared. He'd never seen anything so . . . wonderful! It was as if Christmas had started in this shop and then spread out to cover the whole wide world.

'The Christmas Shop . . .' Peter muttered to himself.

He wondered why he'd never seen it before. True, it was behind the shopping precinct and he usually walked through the precinct not around it, but even so. Peter looked up and down the street. The few other shops in the same row as the Christmas Shop were all boarded up.

Unexpectedly, the shop door opened. A tall portly man with a white beard and a merry twinkle in his eyes stood in the doorway.

'Hello! Come in! Come in!' The shopkeeper beckoned.

'I . . . er . . . don't have much money.' Peter shook his head.

'No matter. Come in.' The shopkeeper turned and held the door open. It was as if there was no doubt in his mind that Peter would enter. Uncertainly, Peter dithered on the pavement. He hadn't intended to go in. He was only window shopping. But the shop looked so warm and inviting and the shopkeeper seemed so friendly. Peter walked into the shop.

And he gasped in amazement!

It was even better inside than it had appeared from outside. It smelt of freshly baked bread and warm cakes and toast and cinnamon and nutmeg and it was so warm, it was as if the sun itself had come for a visit.

'Isn't my shop the best!' smiled the shopkeeper. 'Look around. Feel free. You can pick up anything, touch anything.'

Peter stared at the shopkeeper. He certainly wasn't like any other shopkeeper Peter had ever met. Usually shop-keepers didn't like school kids in their shops and they certainly didn't like them touching things. Peter wandered around the shop, his dark brown eyes wide with delight. Toys and games and Christmas sweets and Christmas treats filled every corner.

Peter's hand curled around the money in his pocket. He could buy all his Christmas presents in here. Peter bent his head to examine a gold and berry-red scarf. That would be perfect for his mum. And maybe the night-blue and yellow scarf for his dad. And he could get that little glass unicorn over there for Chloe. That was just the kind of thing she liked. The strange thing was, none of the items had prices on them.

'H-How much are these woolly scarves?' Peter asked, crossing his fingers in his pockets. 'And how much is that unicorn over there?'

'That depends on who they're for and why you think they'd like them,' answered the shopkeeper.

'The scarves are for my mum and dad and the unicorn is for my sister. Chloe likes things made of glass. She keeps them in her bedroom on the windowsill. And I thought that Mum and Dad could have the scarves to keep them warm.'

'And how much money do you have?' asked the shop-keeper.

Peter took out all the money in his pocket. The shop-keeper checked through it carefully.

'You're lucky,' said the shopkeeper. 'You've got enough for all the things you want.'

'I have? Really?' Peter couldn't believe it.

The shopkeeper smiled and nodded. Peter grinned at him, but slowly his smile faded. He'd buy the scarves for his dad and mum and then what? What good would any present do? Peter could see it now. Mum and Dad opening their presents on Christmas Day.

'Thanks, Peter. That's great,' says Dad.

'Peter, that's wonderful,' says Mum.

And then they'd fling their presents to the back of the chair and start shouting at each other again.

'What's the matter, Peter?' asked the shopkeeper gently.

Peter jumped. He'd been lost in a world of his own.

'It's just that . . . Hang on a second. How did you know my name?' Peter stared.

'It's a little game of mine,' the shopkeeper beamed. 'I like to guess people's names, and nine times out of ten, I get it right.'

Peter was impressed.

'So you were saying?' the shopkeeper prompted.

'I . . . I don't suppose you've got anything in your shop to stop my mum and dad from fighting?' The moment the words were out of his mouth, Peter regretted it. What was he doing? He hadn't told anyone about his mum and dad, not even his best friend Andy. No one knew how things were at home except his sister Chloe, and she didn't talk about it either.

'Oh, I see. Do your mum and dad argue a lot?' asked the shopkeeper.

'All the time,' Peter sighed.

The shopkeeper pursed his lips. 'Hhmm! I think I have just the present you need – for your whole family.'

The shopkeeper went around his brightly coloured counter and disappeared down behind it. Moments later he straightened up, a huge smile on his face and a silver box in his hands.

'These are what you need,' he said.

'What are they?' Peter asked doubtfully.

'Christmas crackers,' announced the shopkeeper proudly. At the disappointed look on Peter's face, he added, 'Ah, but they're not just any crackers. They're magic. Guaranteed to work or your money back.'

'How are they magic?' Peter asked suspiciously.

'The magic only works if they're pulled on Christmas Day, when you're all around the table eating dinner,' explained the shopkeeper.

'But how do they work?'

'It's hard to explain. You have to see the magic for yourself.'

'How much are they?' asked Peter, still doubtful.

Maybe he could buy them and still get the other presents as well.

'I'm afraid they're very expensive because they're magic,' said the shopkeeper. 'They'll cost you all the money you've got, and even then I'm letting you have them cheap.'

Peter thought for a moment. Magic crackers. Crackers that would actually stop Mum and Dad from arguing. They were worth the money if they could do that. He took a deep breath.

'All right, I'll take them,' he said quickly, before he could change his mind.

Peter handed over his money and the shopkeeper handed over the box of eight crackers. Moments later, Peter was out of the shop and running all the way home. Magic crackers! He couldn't wait for Christmas Day.

'I've been in that kitchen since seven o'clock this morning. I think the least you could do is sit at the table with the rest of your family.' Mum's voice dripped with ice.

'I want to watch the end of this film,' Dad argued.

'Typical! You're so selfish,' Mum snapped.

Peter and Chloe looked at each other and sighed. Mum and Dad were at it again. Christmas Day – and they were still arguing.

'Dad, you and Mum and Chloe can open my present now,' Peter said desperately. 'The man in the Christmas

Shop said they should only be opened when we're all sitting round the table eating dinner.'

'Oh, all right then,' Dad grumbled.

'Oh, I see. You'll come to the table if Peter asks you to, but not if I ask you,' sniffed Mum.

'Peter doesn't nag me every two seconds,' Dad said as he sat down at the table.

Chloe shook her head and turned to look out of the window. Peter ran to get the present he'd bought. It was the only one left unopened under the tree. He stood between his mum and dad, putting the present down on the tablecloth. Mum and Dad looked at each other.

'Go on then,' Dad prompted.

'You do it,' said Mum.

'I'll do it,' said Chloe.

She tore off the bright red and yellow wrapping paper.

'It's a box of crackers,' she said, surprised.

'Not just any crackers,' Peter said eagerly. 'They're *magic* crackers!'

'Who told you that?' Mum smiled.

'The man in the Christmas Shop,' Peter replied.

'Well, let's all sit down. Then we can pull them and get on with our dinner,' said Dad, adding under his breath, 'And maybe then I can get back to my film.'

But the moment they all sat down, something peculiar began to happen. A strange feeling settled over the dinner table. A hopeful, expectant feeling — as if, in spite of themselves, everyone was waiting for something terrific, amazing *and* spectacular to happen all at once. The noise from the telly was just a distant hum at the other end of the room. Light, like warm spring sunshine, came from everyone, smiling at everyone else as they watched Dad place two crackers beside each plate. Chloe held out her cracker to Dad. Peter held his Christmas cracker out to Mum.

'One! Two! Three!' they all shouted.

Bang! Pop! The sound of exploding crackers filled the room. Chloe and Peter got the biggest parts of the crackers. They both peered down into them.

'They're . . . they're *empty!*' Chloe exclaimed.

'No! They can't be,' frowned Mum.

'See for yourself,' said Chloe, handing over her cracker.

Peter couldn't believe it. Empty . . . When he remembered the smiling, friendly face of the jolly man with the white beard in the Christmas Shop, he just *couldn't* believe it. That man wouldn't take his money and sell him a box of *nothing* — Peter was sure he wouldn't. And yet . . . and yet, his cracker was empty. Just an empty roll covered with some glossy paper and nothing else. No hats. No jokes. No gifts. Nothing.

'Maybe there were just two duff ones in the box,' Mum suggested.

Mum and Dad pulled their crackers next. The same

thing happened. They were empty. Chloe and Peter pulled crackers five and six at the same time as Mum and Dad pulled crackers seven and eight.

They were all empty.

Peter examined each one, hoping against hope that they'd got it wrong or it was a trick – but it wasn't. Peter looked at Chloe, then Mum and Dad – and burst into tears. He couldn't help it.

'The shopkeeper told me they were magic crackers,' Peter sobbed to Mum and Dad. 'I only bought them because he said they would make you stop arguing with each other. He promised me they were magic. He *promised* me . . .'

Dad stared. Mum's mouth fell open.

'You . . . you bought them – because of *us*?' Dad asked, aghast.

Peter sniffed and nodded.

'Never mind, Peter.' Chloe put her arm around her younger brother's shoulder. 'Besides, nothing would stop Mum and Dad from fighting. Not even a real box of magic crackers.' And with that, Chloe burst into tears too.

'Chloe! Peter!' Mum and Dad ran around the table to hug Peter and Chloe to them. 'We had no idea we were quarrelling that much.'

'And we had no idea we were upsetting both of you so much,' said Dad.

But Peter and Chloe couldn't stop crying.

'I'll tell you what,' said Mum. 'Let's make our own Christmas crackers. All this food will stay warm in the oven until we've finished.'

'Terrific idea.' Dad went over to the telly and switched it off. 'We'll make the hats first,' Dad continued. 'Out of newspaper.'

Dad and Mum showed Peter and Chloe how to make sailor hats out of newspaper. That took about five minutes. Then they all sat down for dinner. Over dinner, everyone had to tell the worst jokes they knew, like, 'How do you make an apple puff? Chase it round the garden!' and 'Why did the elephant cross the road? Because it was the chicken's day off!' Dad's joke was 'Why did silly Billy stand on a ladder when he was learning to sing? So he could reach the high notes!' And Mum's joke was ancient but she was still proud of it! 'How do you make a Swiss Roll? Push him down a hill!' Chloe told a joke that Peter didn't get until Mum explained it. 'How do you tell how old a telephone is? Count its rings!' (Mum explained that you could tell the age of a tree by counting the rings through its trunk.) Everyone got Peter's joke. 'Why are vampires crazy? Because they're often bats!' And when anyone ran out of jokes, they made them up, which was even funnier!

After dinner when everyone was eating Christmas

pudding, Mum grabbed Dad and whispered in his ear. Suddenly they both dashed off upstairs with the empty crackers. Ten minutes later they reappeared with the various ends of each cracker now glued together.

'Cracker time!' said Mum. And she held out a cracker to Chloe.

They both pulled.

'POP!' shouted Mum.

Chloe looked inside the cracker and there was one of Mum's old bangles – the gold and blue one which had always been Chloe's favourite.

'Your turn,' said Dad, holding out a cracker to Peter. They both shouted, 'BANG!'

Peter looked inside the cracker. There was a pig made of lego bricks. At least, that's what Peter thought it was.

'It's not a pig. It's a rocket!' said Dad indignantly.

Mum started to giggle. 'I told you it looked more like a pig, dear,' she said.

They 'popped' the rest of the crackers. They all had very silly, very tacky, very wonderful presents in them.

'Who needs rotten, mouldy old crackers?' asked Dad. 'We can do it all ourselves.'

'And they're much better too,' Mum agreed. 'It's just a shame that Peter got conned out of his money. Where did you say the shop was?'

'Behind the precinct. All the other shops on the same street were boarded up,' Peter replied.

'There aren't any shops behind the precinct. The last one closed down over a year ago,' Dad frowned.

'There's one still open. It's called the Christmas Shop,' said Peter.

Mum and Dad looked at each other. They both shrugged.

'Never mind. I'd say they were the best crackers we've ever had,' smiled Mum. 'My jaw still aches from laughing at all those terrible jokes.'

'Those crackers were ... a box of magic,' said Dad, giving Mum a cuddle.

Later that night, as Peter lay in bed, he still couldn't quite believe what had happened. Mum and Dad hadn't argued once since the crackers had been pulled. In fact, it was the most wonderful day they'd all had in a long, long time. The only cloud was the shopkeeper who'd sold Peter the crackers in the first place. Peter still didn't want to believe that the shopkeeper was a crook who had deliberately diddled him out of his money.

A strange tinkling-clinking came from across the room, followed by a plopping sound. Peter sat up and frowned. What was that? He switched on his bedside light. There it was again – the same strange noise. And it seemed to be coming from his chair over by the window. Over the back of the chair were the jumper and the pair of trousers Peter had worn on Christmas Eve. That strange noise couldn't be coming from them – could it? Swallowing hard, Peter got up and tiptoed across to the chair.

Tinkle! Clinkle! Plop!

There it was again! Peter took a deep breath, counted to three, then quickly pulled the chair to one side. More money fell out of his trouser pockets and plopped on to the carpet. Peter's eyes goggled! Where had all that money come from? He scooped up the money on the floor, then picked up his trousers and dug into his pockets. There was more money inside them. He counted it all very carefully. It was the exact amount of money he had paid for the Christmas crackers . . .

Peter sat down on his bed and stared down at the money in his hand. What was going on? He shook his head and looked around the room hoping for some clue. Had Mum and Dad done it? Had they put the money in his pockets to make up for him losing his money in the Christmas Shop? But they didn't know exactly how much he'd paid for the crackers. And now here he was, with the exact same coins in his hand.

Then something else caught his eye. There on his bedside table, were all the Christmas cards he'd received from his friends. At the front was the card he'd got from his best friend Andy. Peter gasped and stared so hard, his eyes began to ache.

The face on the card . . .

Peter had seen that face before – in the Christmas Shop. The shopkeeper and Father Christmas were one and the same person . . . Peter picked up the card and studied it. The shopkeeper *was* Father Christmas. Peter was sure of it. And that would explain how he'd got his money back. Which meant only one thing . . .

The Christmas crackers *were* magic after all.

'Thank you,' Peter whispered to the Christmas card.

And he was sure that on the card, the smiling face of Father Christmas winked at him.

Christmas Is Coming

(from *The Country Child*)

ALISON UTTLEY

At Christmas the wind ceased to moan. Snow lay thick on the fields and the woods cast blue shadows across it. The fir trees were like sparkling, gem-laden Christmas trees, the only ones Susan had ever seen. The orchard, with the lacy old boughs outlined with snow, was a grove of fairy trees. The woods were enchanted, exquisite, the trees were holy, and anything harmful had shrunken to a thin wisp and had retreated into the depths.

The fields lay with their unevennesses gone and paths obliterated, smooth white slopes criss-crossed by black lines running up to the woods. More than ever the farm seemed under a spell, like a toy in the forest, with little wooden animals and men; a brown horse led by a stiff little red-scarfed man to a yellow stable door; round, white, woolly sheep clustering round a blue trough of orange mangolds; red cows drinking from a square, white trough, and returning to a painted cow-house.

Footprints were everywhere on the snow, rabbits and foxes, blackbirds, pheasants and partridges, trails of small paws, the mark of a brush, and the long feet of the cock pheasant and the tip-mark of his tail.

A jay flew out of the wood like a blue flashing diamond and came to the grass-plot for bread. A robin entered the house and hopped under the table while Susan sat very still and her father sprinkled crumbs on the floor.

Rats crouched outside the window, peeping out of the walls with gleaming eyes, seizing the birds' crumbs and scraps, and slowly lolloping back again.

Red squirrels ran along the walls to the back door, close to the window, to eat the crumbs on the bench where the milk cans froze. Every wild animal felt that a truce had come with the snow, and they visited the house where there was food in plenty, and sat with paws uplifted and noses twitching.

For the granaries were full, it had been a prosperous year, and there was food for everyone. Not like the year before when there was so little hay that Mr Garland had to buy a stack in February. Three large haystacks as big as houses stood in the stackyard, thatched evenly and straight by Job Fletcher, who was the best thatcher for many a mile. Great mounds showed where the roots were buried. The brick-lined pit was filled with grains and in the barns were stores of corn.

The old brew-house was full of logs of wood, piled high against the walls, cut from trees which the wind had blown down. The coal-house with its strong ivied walls, part of the old fortress, had been stored with coal brought many a mile in the blaze of summer; twenty tons lay under the snow.

On the kitchen walls hung the sides of bacon and from hooks in the ceiling dangled great hams and shoulders. Bunches of onions were twisted in the pantry and barn, and an empty cow-house was stored with potatoes for immediate use.

The floor of the apple chamber was covered with apples, rosy apples, little yellow ones, like cowslip balls, wizenedy apples with withered, wrinkled cheeks, fat, well-fed smooth-faced apples, and immense green cookers, pointed like a house, which would burst in the oven and pour out a thick cream of the very essence of apples.

Even the cheese chamber had its cheeses this year, for there had been too much milk for the milkman, and the cheese presses had been put into use again. Some of them were Christmas cheese, with layers of sage running through the middles like green ribbons.

Stone jars like those in which the forty thieves hid stood on the pantry floor, filled with white lard, and balls of fat tied up in bladders hung from the hooks. Along the broad shelves round the walls were pots of jam, blackberry and apple, from the woods and orchard, Victoria plum from the trees on house and barn, blackcurrant from the garden, and redcurrant jelly, damson cheese from the half-wild ancient trees which grew everywhere, leaning over walls, dropping their blue fruit on paths and walls, in pigsty and orchard, in field and water trough, so that Susan thought they were wild as hips and haws.

Pickles and spices filled old brown pots decorated with crosses and flowers, like the pitchers and crocks of Will Shakespeare's time.

In the little dark wine chamber under the stairs were bottles of elderberry wine, purple, thick, and sweet, and golden cowslip wine, and hot ginger, some of them many years old, waiting for the winter festivities.

There were dishes piled with mince pies on the shelves of the larder, and a row of plum puddings with their white calico caps, and strings of sausages, and round pats of butter, with swans and cows and wheat-ears printed upon them.

Everyone who called at the farm had to eat and drink at Christmas-tide.

A few days before Christmas, Mr Garland and Dan took a bill-hook and knife and went into the woods to cut branches of scarlet-berried holly. They tied them together with ropes and dragged them down over the fields to the barn. Mr Garland cut a bough of mistletoe from the ancient hollow hawthorn which leaned over the wall by the orchard, and thick clumps of dark-berried ivy from the walls.

Indoors, Mrs Garland and Susan and Becky polished and rubbed and cleaned the furniture and brasses, so that everything glowed and glittered. They decorated every room, from the kitchen where every lustre jug had its sprig in its mouth, every brass candlestick had its chaplet, every copper saucepan and preserving-pan had its wreath of shining berries and leaves, through the hall, which was a bower of green, to the two parlours which were festooned and hung with holly and boughs of fir, and ivy berries dipped in red raddle, left over from sheep marking.

Holly decked every picture and ornament. Sprays hung over the bacon and twisted round the hams and herb bunches. The clock carried a crown on his head, and every dish-cover had a little sprig. Susan kept an eye on the lonely forgotten humble things, the jelly moulds and colanders and nutmeg-grater, and made them happy with glossy leaves. Everything seemed to speak, to ask for its morsel of greenery, and she tried to leave out nothing.

On Christmas Eve fires blazed in the kitchen and

parlour and even in the bedrooms. Becky ran from room to room with the red-hot salamander which she stuck between the bars to make a blaze, and Mrs Garland took the copper warming-pan filled with glowing cinders from the kitchen fire and rubbed it between the sheets of all the beds. Susan had come down to her cosy tiny room with thick curtains at the window, and a fire in the big fireplace. Flames roared up the chimneys as Dan carried in the logs and Becky piled them on the blaze. The wind came back and tried to get in, howling at the key holes, but all the shutters were cottered and the doors shut. The horses and mares stood in the stables, warm and happy, with nodding heads. The cows slept in the cow-houses, the sheep in the open sheds. Only Rover stood at the door of his kennel, staring up at the sky, howling to the dog in the moon, and then he too turned and lay down in his straw.

In the middle of the kitchen ceiling there hung the kissing-bunch, the best and brightest pieces of holly made in the shape of a large ball, which dangled from the hook. Silver and gilt drops, crimson bells, blue glass trumpets, bright oranges and red polished apples, peeped and glittered through the glossy leaves. Little flags of all nations, but chiefly Turkish for some unknown reason, stuck out like quills on a hedgehog. The lamp hung near, and every little berry, every leaf, every pretty ball and apple had a tiny yellow flame reflected in its heart.

Twisted candles hung down, yellow, red, and blue, unlighted but gay, and on either side was a string of paper lanterns.

Mrs Garland climbed on a stool and nailed on the wall the Christmas texts, 'God bless our Home', 'God is Love', 'Peace be on this House', 'A Happy Christmas and a Bright New Year'.

So the preparations were made. Susan hung up her stocking at the foot of the bed and fell asleep. But soon singing roused her and she sat, bewildered. Yes, it was the carol singers.

Outside under the stars she could see the group of men and women, with lanterns throwing beams across the paths and on to the stable door. One man stood apart beating time, another played a fiddle and another had a flute. The rest sang in four parts the Christmas hymns, 'While Shepherds Watched', 'O Come, all Ye faithful', and 'Hark the Herald Angels Sing'.

There was the Star, Susan could see it twinkling and bright in the dark boughs with their white frosted layers; and there was the stable. She watched the faces half-lit by lanterns. A bright light flickered across the snow as the door was flung wide open. Then a bang, and Susan went back to bed. Christmas Eve was nearly over, but tomorrow was Christmas Day, the best day in all the year.

Schnitzle, Schnotzle, Schnootzle

RUTH SAWYER

The Tirol straddles the Alps and reaches one hand into Italy and another into Austria. There are more mountains in the Tirol than you can count and every Alp has its story.

Long ago, some say on the Brenner-Alp, some say on the Mitterwald-Alp, there lived the king of all the goblins of the Tirol, and his name was Laurin. King Laurin. His kingdom was under the earth, and all the gold and silver of the mountains he owned. He had a daughter, very young and very lovely, not at all like her father, who had a bulbous nose, big ears and a squat figure, and looked as old as the mountains. She loved flowers and was sad that none grew inside her father's kingdom.

'I want a garden of roses — red roses, pink roses, blush roses, flame roses, shell roses, roses like the sunrise and the sunset.' This she said one day to her father. And the king laughed and said she should have just such a garden. They would roof it with crystal, so that the sun would pour into the depths of the kingdom and make the roses grow lovely and fragrant. The garden was planted and every rare and exquisite rose bloomed in it. And so much colour spread upwards on the mountains around that the snow caught it and the *mortals* living in the valley pointed at it with wonder. 'What is it that makes our Alps so rosy, so glowing?' they asked. And they spoke of it ever after as the alpen-glow.

I have told you this that you might know what kind of goblin King Laurin was. He was merry, and he liked to play pranks and have fun. He liked to do abroad into the valleys where the *mortals* lived, or pop into a herdsman's hut halfway up the mountain. There were two men who said they had seen him — that small squat figure with a bulbous nose and big ears, gambolling with the goats on a summer day. And now I begin my story. It is an old one that Tirolèse mothers like to tell to their children.

Long ago there lived in one of the valleys a very poor cobbler indeed. His wife had died and left him with three children, little boys all of them – Fritzl, Franzl, and Hansl. They lived in a hut so small there was only one room in it, and in that room was the cobbler's bench, a hearth for cooking, a big bed full of straw, and on the wall racks for a few dishes, and, of course, there was a table with a settle and some stools. They needed few dishes or pans, for there was never much to cook or eat. Sometimes the cobbler would mend the Sunday shoes of a farmer, and then there was good goat's milk to drink. Sometimes he would mend the holiday shoes of the baker, and then there was the good long crusty loaf of bread to eat. And sometimes he mended the shoes of the butcher, and then there was the good stew, cooked with meat in the pot, and noodles, leeks, and herbs. When the cobbler gathered the little boys around the table and they had said their grace, he would laugh and clap his hands and sometimes even dance.

'Ha-ha!' he would shout. 'Today we have the good . . . what? Ah-h . . . today we eat . . . Schnitzle, Schnotzle, and Schnootzle!'

With that he would swing the kettle off the hook and fill every bowl brimming full, and Fritzl, Franzl, and Hansl would eat until they had had enough. Ach, those were the good days – the days of having Schnitzle, Schnotzle, and Schnootzle. Of course, the cobbler was making up nonsense and nothing else, but the stew tasted so much better because of the nonsense.

Now a year came, with every month following his brother on leaden feet. The little boys and the cobbler heard the month of March tramp out and April tramp in. They heard June tramp out and July tramp in. And every month marched heavier than his brother. And that was because war was among them again. War, with workers taking up their guns and leaving mothers and children to care for themselves as best they could; and there was scant to pay even a poor cobbler for mending shoes. The whole village shuffled to church with the soles flapping and the heels lopsided, and the eyelets and buttons and straps quite gone.

Summer — that was not so bad. But winter came and covered up the good earth, and gone were the roots, the berries, the sorrel, and the corn. The tramp of November going out and December coming in was very loud indeed. The little boys were quite sure that the two months shook the hut as they passed each other on the mountainside.

As Christmas grew near, the little boys began to wonder if there would be any feast for them, if there would be the good father dancing about the room and laughing. 'Ha-ha', and singing, 'Ho-ho', and saying: 'Now, this being Christmas Day we have the good . . . what?' And this time the little boys knew that they would never wait for their father to say it; they would shout themselves: 'We know — it is the good Schnitzle, Schnotzle, and Schnootzle!'

Ach, how very long it was since their father had mended shoes for the butcher! Surely — surely — there would be need again soon, with Christmas so near.

At last came the Eve of Christmas. The little boys climbed along the beginnings of the Brenner-Alp, looking for faggots. The trees had shed so little that year; every branch was green and grew fast to its tree, so few twigs had snapped, so little was there of dead, dried bush to fill their arms.

Their father came in when they had a small fire started, blowing his whiskers free of icicles, slapping his arms about his big body, trying to put warmth back into it. 'Na-na, nobody will have a shoes mended today. I have asked everyone. Still, there is good news. The soldiers are marching into the village. The inn is full. They will have boots that need mending, those soldiers. You will see.' He pinched a cheek of each little boy; he winked at them and nodded his head. 'You shall see — tonight I will come home with . . . what?'

'Schnitzle, Schnotzle, and Schnootzle,' they shouted together, those three.

So happy they were they forgot there was nothing to eat for supper — not a crust, not a slice of cold porridge-pudding, not the smallest sup of goat's milk. 'Will the soldiers have money to pay you?' asked Fritzl, the oldest.

'Not the soldiers, perhaps, but the captains. There might even be a general. I will mend the boots of the soldiers for nothing, for after all what day is coming tomorrow? They fight for us, those soldiers; we mend for them, *ja*? But a general — he will have plenty of money.'

The boys stood about while their father put all his tools, all his pieces of leather into a rucksack; while he wound and wound and wound the woollen scarf about his neck, while he pulled the cap far down on his head. 'It will be a night to freeze the ears off you,' he said. 'Now bolt the door after me, keep the fire burning with a little at a time; and climb into the straw bed and pull the quilt over you. And let no one in!'

He was gone. They bolted the door; they put a little on the fire; they climbed into the big bed, putting Hansl, the smallest, in the middle. They pulled up the quilt, such a thin quilt to keep out so much cold! Straight and still and close together they lay, looking up at the little spot of light the fire made on the ceiling, watching their breath go upwards in icy spurts. With the going of the sun the wind rose. First it whispered: it whispered of good fires in big chimneys; it whispered of the pines on the mountainsides; it whispered of the snow loosening and sliding over the glaciers. Then it began to blow: it blew hard, it blew quarrelsome, it blew cold and colder. And at last it roared. It roared its wintry breath through the cracks in the walls and under the door. And Fritzl, Franzl, and Hansl drew closer together and shivered.

'Whee . . . ooh . . . bang, bang! Whee . . . ooh . . . bang, bang!'

'Is it the wind or someone knocking?' asked Franzl.

'It is the wind,' said Fritzl.

'Whee . . . ooh . . . knock, knock!'

'Is it the wind or someone knocking?' asked Hansl.

'It is the wind and someone knocking!' said Fritzl.

He rolled out of the bed and went to the window. It looked out directly on the path to the door. 'Remember what our father said: do not open it,' said Franzl.

But Fritzl looked and looked. Close to the hut, beaten against it by the wind, stood a little man no bigger than Hansl. He was pounding on the door. Now they could hear him calling: 'Let me in! I tell you, let me in!'

'Oh don't, don't!' cried Hansl.

'I must,' said Fritzl. 'He looks very cold. The wind is tearing at him as a wolf tears at a young lamb', and with that he drew the bolt and into the hut skipped the oddest little man they had ever seen. He had a great peaked cap tied on to his head with deer-thongs. He had a round red face out of which stuck a bulbous nose, like a fat plum on a pudding. He had big ears. And his teeth were chattering so hard they made the stools to dance. He shook his fist at the three little boys. 'Ach, kept me waiting.

Wanted to keep all the good food, all the good fire to yourselves? Na-na, that is no kind of hospitality.'

He looked over at the little bit of a fire on the hearth, making hardly any heat in the hut. He looked at the empty table, not a bowl set or a spoon beside it. He took up the big pot, peered into it, turned it upside down to make sure nothing was clinging to the bottom, set it down with a bang. 'So — you have already eat it all. Greedy boys. But if you have saved no feast for me, you can at least warm me.' With that he climbed into the big straw-bed with Franzl and Hansl, with his cap still tied under his chin. Fritzl tried to explain that they had not been greedy, that there had never been any food, not for days, to speak of. But he was too frightened of the little man, of his eyes as sharp and blue as ice, of his mouth so grumbling.

'Roll over, roll over,' the little man was shouting at the two in the bed. 'Can't you see I have no room? Roll over and give me half of the quilt.'

Fritzl saw that he was pushing his brothers out of the bed. 'Na-na,' he said, trying to make peace with their guest. 'They are little, those two. There is room for all if we but lie quiet.' And he started to climb into the bed himself, pulling gently at the quilt that there might be a corner for him.

But the little man bounced and rolled about, shouting: 'Give me room, give me more quilt. Can't you see I'm cold? I call this poor hospitality to bring a stranger inside your door, give him nothing to eat, and then grudge him bed and covering to keep him warm.' He dug his elbow into the side of skinny little Hansl.

'Ouch!' cried the boy.

Fritzl began to feel angry. 'Sir,' he said, 'sir, I pray you to be gentle with my little brother. And I am sorry there has been nothing to give you. But our father, the cobbler, has gone to mend shoes for the soldiers. When he returns we look for food. Truly, this is a night to feast and to share. SO if you will but lit still until he comes I can promise you . . .'

The little man rolled over and stuck his elbow into Fritzl's ribs. 'Promise — Promise. Na-na, what good is a promise? Come, get out of bed and give me your place.' He drew up his knees, put his feet in the middle of Fritzl's back and pushed with a great strength. The next moment the boy was spinning across the room. 'There you go,' roared the little man after him. 'If you must keep warm turn cartwheels, turn them fast.'

For a moment Fritzl stood sullenly by the small speck of fire. He felt bruised and very angry. He looked over at the bed. Sure enough, the greedy little man had rolled himself up in the quilt, leaving only a short corner of it for the two younger boys. He had taken more than half of the straw for himself, and was even then pushing and digging at Hansl. He saw Franzl raise himself up and take the place of his littlest brother, so that he should get the digs.

Barr . . . it was cold! Before he knew it Fritzl was doing as he had been told, turning cartwheels around the room. He had rounded the table and was coming toward the bed when – plop! Plop – plop – plop! Things were falling out of his pockets every time his feet swung high over his head. Plop – plop – plop! The two younger boys were sitting up in bed. It was their cries of astonishment which brought Fritzl's feet back to the floor again, to stay. In a circle about the room, he had left behind him a golden trail of oranges. Such oranges – big as two fists! And sprinkled everywhere between were commits wrapped in gold and silver paper. Fritzl stood and gaped at them.

'Here, you, get out and keep warm yourself!' shouted the little man as he dug Franzl in the ribs. 'Cartwheels for you, boy!' And the next minute Franzl was hurling in cartwheels about the room. Plop – plop – plop – things were dropping out of his pockets: Christmas buns, Christmas cookies covered with icing, with plums, with anise and caraway seeds.

The little man was now digging Hansl in the ribs. 'Lazy boy, greedy boy. Think you can have the bed to yourself now? Na-na, I'll have it! Out you go!' and he put his feet against the littlest boy's back and pushed him on to the floor. 'Cartwheels . . .' he began; but Fritzl, forgetting his amazement at what was happening, shouted: 'But, sir, he is too little. He cannot turn . . .'

'Hold him up in the corner, then. You keep warmer when your heels are higher than your head. Step lively there. Take a leg, each of you, and be quick about it.'

So angry did the little man seem, so fiery and determined, that Fritzl and Franzl hurried their little brother over to the chimney corner, stood him on his head and each held a leg. Donner and Blitzen! What happened then! Whack – whack – whickety-whack! Whack – whack– whickety-whack! Pelting the floor like hail against the roof came silver and gold pieces, all pouring out of Hansl's pockets.

Fritzl began to shout, Franzl began to dance. Hansl began to shout: 'Let me down, let me down!' When they did the three little boys danced around the pile, taking hands, singing 'Tra-la-la', and 'Fiddle-de-dee', and 'Ting-a-ling-a-ling', until their breath was gone and they could dance no longer. They looked over at the bed and Fritzl was opening his mouth to say: 'Now, if you please, sir, we can offer you some Christmas cheer . . .' But the bed was empty, the quilt lay in a heap on the floor. The little man had gone.

The three little boys were gathering up the things on the floor – putting oranges into the big wooden bowl, buns and cookies on to the two platters, silver and gold pieces into this dish and that. And right in the midst of it in came their father, stamping, puffing in through the door. He had brought bread, he had brought milk, he had brought meat for the good stew – and noodles.

Such a wonder, such a clapping of hands, such a singing as they worked to get ready the Christmas feast! Fritzl began the story about their Christmas guest; Franzl told it mid-through; but little Hansl finished, making his brothers stand him in the corner again on his head to show just how it was that all the silver and gold had tumbled out of his pockets.

'Na-na,' said the cobbler, 'we are the lucky ones. I did not know it was true; always I thought it was a tale the grandfathers told the children. The saying goes that King Laurin comes every year at the Christmas to one hut – one family – to play his tricks and share his treasure hoard.'

'He was a very ugly little man,' said Hansl. 'He dug us in our ribs and took all the bed for himself.'

'That was the king – that is the way he plays at being fierce. Say a special Christmas grace, then draw up the stools. Ah-h . . . what have we to eat?'

The little boys shouted the answer all together: 'Schnitzle – Schnotzle – Schnootzle!'

Mrs Mudd's Cross Christmas

ALISON PRINCE

'Oh, no,' said Boris. 'Not Mrs Mudd. Do we have to? She's awful.'

'I know,' said his mother. 'But it's Christmas, Boris. She'd be sitting there next door all by herself – we'll have to ask her.'

Boris nodded gloomily. 'S'pose so,' he said. 'But she grumbles all the time.'

'You'll never notice, not with so many other people in the house,' his mother said. 'One more won't make any difference.'

Boris hoped she was right, but he doubted it. You couldn't help noticing someone as cross as Mrs Mudd.

Christmas came. The house was hung with gold stars and paper chains and all the windows were covered with rather untidy snowflakes which Boris's little sister Masha had cut out of paper. People started to arrive.

Uncle Vodka was first, with his huge dog called Peter the Great, and both of them kissed everyone. Boris managed to avoid being kissed by Uncle Vodka. He didn't mind the dog so much – at least it didn't have a beard.

Then there was Tanya and the Tribe, who all came tumbling out of their big old car together with Christmas presents and nappies and chocolates and somebody's new tricycle, carried by Tanya's Anatoli. Uncle Vodka's real name was Anatoli as well, which was why they called him something else.

Grandma and Grandpa were already there, because they were staying in the house. They'd come over from Russia and didn't speak any English, but they smiled a lot.

And there was Mrs Mudd. She came to the front door instead of round the back like everyone else, and nobody found her until Boris and his father went to tie a holly wreath to the knocker.

'I rang,' she said, 'but nobody came.'

'The bell doesn't work,' said Boris.

Mrs Mudd glared at him and said, 'It's perfectly easy to fix.'

Boris's father looked surprised and said, 'Is it really?' But then, he played the violin and didn't do practical things like fixing doorbells.

Mrs Mudd came into the kitchen and gave Boris's mother a very heavy cake. Then she gave Masha and Boris hand-knitted woolly hats that were a bit big, and they went upstairs to try them on in front of the bedroom mirror and make silly faces, and laughed a lot. When they came back, Mrs Mudd was sitting in a chair with a glass of fizzy water in her hand, still looking cross. She was wearing her usual shapeless trousers and an unravelling jersey that was mostly brown, and she was staring suspiciously at a painted wooden egg which Grandma had given her. 'What's it for?' she asked.

'*Shto?*' enquired Grandma. Someone translated for her, and she beamed and said, 'For looking at, of course. You like it?'

Boris told Mrs Mudd what Grandma had said.

'Very foreign, isn't it?' said Mrs Mudd.

'She thinks it's beautiful,' Boris told Grandma, 'and she says thank you very much.' He was quite glad when Masha appeared and tried to give Mrs Mudd a party hat with a tall green feather.

'Hats give me a headache,' said Mrs Mudd.

'How *awful*,' said Masha, who was going to be an actress when she grew up. She clutched her own head in both hands and staggered about, moaning, 'Oh, my head, my head.'

Peter the Great began to howl and one of Tanya's Tribe burst into tears, and Mrs Mudd said, 'Now look what you've done.'

'Here's to peace and friendship between all people,' said Uncle Vodka, raising his glass. 'What have you got there – gin?'

'Water,' said Mrs Mudd. 'I don't hold with drink.'

'Oh,' said Uncle Vodka. 'Well, peace and friendship anyway. What's your name?'

'Mudd,' said Mrs Mudd.

Tanya's Anatoli began to laugh uncontrollably and fled into the kitchen to be thumped on the back by Boris's mother. Uncle Vodka said, 'No, I mean your first name. Nobody can go around being called Mudd, can they? Cheers.'

'Violet,' said Mrs Mudd.

'And very nice too,' said Uncle Vodka.

They seemed to be getting on all right, so Boris left them to it. In the kitchen, Tanya's Anatoli had recovered a bit and was wiping his eyes. 'That woman!' he said. 'Who on earth is she?'

'Our next-door neighbour,' Boris told him. 'I knew we shouldn't have asked her.'

'Boris, quiet,' scolded his mother, ramming something through the mincer. 'She's all right.'

'She's terrible,' said Anatoli. 'I'm not going back in there. Can't I help with the cooking?'

'There's no room,' Boris's mother said — which was true, because the kitchen already had Grandma in it, peeling beetroot, and Tanya feeding a baby and several of her Tribe busy with their new colouring books open on the table among the onions and flour, and Grandpa just sitting. 'If you really want to help, go and amuse Mrs Mudd.'

'Impossible,' said Anatoli. 'I'd rather change nappies.' And he picked up the nearest of the Tribe, who was eating a pot of raspberry jam, and sniffed hopefully at its trousers.

There seemed to be food absolutely everywhere, Boris thought. They had unloaded box after box of it from the big old car, and Uncle Vodka had arrived with a lot of bottles and a large fish. Grandma had lugged a huge jar of bottled plums all the way from Moscow and Grandpa had gone mad in the supermarket round the corner, buying things he thought were rare and wonderful, like Mars bars and Hula Hoops and tinned spaghetti.

Boris's mother, of course, had been cooking for days, doing complicated things with cabbage leaves and meat balls and sour cream. 'I want Grandma and Grandpa to feel at home,' she'd explained. 'A real Russian meal.'

Mrs Mudd didn't feel at home at all. After quite a long time, when the kitchen was smelling wonderfully of apricots and turkey and onions and mushrooms, she came in and said, 'Shall I do the sprouts?'

Everyone looked at each other.

'*Kak* SPROUT?' asked Grandma, who was keen on learning English words.

'Little cabbages,' Boris explained. 'I don't know what they are in Russian, we never had them until we came here.'

'I mean, time's getting on, isn't it?' said Mrs Mudd. 'If you'd just like to give me a knife and clear some of the children off the table.'

'No, please,' said Boris's mother with her biggest smile. 'Sit down, relax, OK? Some more water? Where is Anatoli, he could play the piano. Masha, why don't you read Mrs Mudd one of your poems?'

'I'll read the one about the squashed worm,' said Masha.

'No, a nice one, Masha. Please, Masha!'

But Masha had gone to get her writing book, her fingers pressed to her forehead in a poetic way. Mrs Mudd said, 'Well, I just thought I'd offer,' and went back to her chair looking crosser than ever.

Masha came back with a large black notebook and started to read her poem about the worm. Mrs Mudd shut her eyes. Uncle Vodka said, 'Here's to poetry!' and raised his glass again, but she didn't open them.

Tanya's Anatoli sat down at the piano and Boris's father Ivan got his violin out and they started to play something very soulful. 'Brahms,' said Uncle Vodka. 'They must be getting hungry. They'll play something more cheerful after lunch.'

Mrs Mudd said, 'I certainly hope so.'

Masha finished her worm poem and began one about a road accident.

It was about four o'clock before lunch looked like happening. Nobody minded, because they'd all been eating salted fish and peanuts and the packets of things Grandpa had bought, and Tanya had made Ivan and Anatoli play something cheerful – but Mrs Mudd kept looking at her watch and sighing.

Boris's mother said, 'We'll need the extra section in the table with so many of us. Ivan, can you get it?'

Ivan stopped playing and said, 'Get what?'

Everyone explained all over again, and Ivan and Grandpa went upstairs and came back with a big table-top and a bag of props and struts. 'Where do we put it?' Ivan asked.

'In the middle,' said Tanya's Anatoli. 'You pull the table apart, you see, and this bit goes in the middle, to fill the gap. There are twisty things underneath to hold it, and some screws. Then the table's much bigger.'

Everyone pushed and hauled at the table's legs and its two outside bits. 'Mind your fingers,' Boris's mother said to Ivan. 'You're playing in a concert in three days' time, remember. You'd better leave this to us.'

'Oh, good,' said Ivan, helping himself to a fried sprat. 'M'm, these are nice. Would you like one, Mrs Mudd?'

'No, thank you,' said Mrs Mudd. 'Did anybody do the sprouts?'

Nobody answered. People were crawling under the table, trying to see how it worked, and Peter the Great thought it was a game and started to bark. Grandpa shouted at him in Russian and Tanya told him not to use words like that in front of the children, and Uncle Vodka got his fingers squashed.

'I think this twisty thing has to go in there,' said Boris's mother, peering underneath. 'Push your bit further over, Anatoli. No, not Grandpa's bit. Just hold it like that while the children – Sasha, don't let go, darling. Oh, Kolya, did it hit you on the head? Oh, sweetheart, don't cry. Ivan, could you give him a sprat?'

Kolya said he didn't want a sprat, he wanted a packet of Hula Hoops, and Grandpa tore one open for him, beaming proudly.

'He won't want his dinner,' said Mrs Mudd, and added darkly, 'if it ever comes.'

At last the table was together, with nobody holding it up. 'Isn't it lovely and big!' said Masha. 'Can I dance on it?'

'Of course you can't dance on it,' Boris said. 'Don't be stupid, we're all going to eat.'

Masha gave the table a little shake and said, 'It feels a bit wobbly — perhaps I'd better not.'

'Leave it alone, Masha,' said her mother. 'Come and put some knives and forks out for me. Mrs Mudd, do come and sit down.'

Mrs Mudd pulled her chair to the table and watched doubtfully as the dishes arrived. 'What is it?' she asked.

'*Zakuski*,' said Boris. 'Starters. Like, little cheese fritters and slices of sausage and pickled cucumbers and fish and — well, everything, really.'

'I suppose you're used to it,' said Mrs Mudd, and took a small piece of tomato.

'Here's to international understanding!' said Uncle Vodka. Everyone clinked glasses and Mrs Mudd said, 'Yes, I suppose so,' and took a sip of water.

Everyone ate lots of *zakuski* and more toasts were drunk — to the cook, to everyone's health, to friendship, to Mrs Mudd, to babies, to the dog. But, as Boris had said, that was just starters, and the main part of the meal was still to come. They all helped to carry in the dishes — stuffed cabbage leaves, roast potatoes, carrots stewed with raisins and prunes, beetroot, glazed onions, red peppers, the turkey itself, hot pickled cucumber, aubergines, mushrooms –

'You forgot the sprouts,' said Mrs Mudd.

'Um, well, no,' Boris's mother admitted as she held the turkey on its huge dish, wafting a smell of apricots and garlic. 'Actually, I wasn't planning to have sprouts.'

'For goodness' sake!' said Mrs Mudd. 'I'd have brought you some from the garden, if you'd just said.'

'Here's to gardens!' shouted Uncle Vodka, a little desperately.

'Make a space for this turkey,' said Boris's mother. People moved things aside, she lowered the great dish – and the table collapsed. It fell down in the middle and everything slid together in a great heap of plates and forks and knives and Christmas crackers and food. Luckily, Peter the Great happened to be underneath, which stopped things from going all the way to the floor, but it was a terrible confusion and spillage and everyone shrieked and screamed and grabbed at things. Boris's mother made a dive for the turkey, Masha and Grandma burst into tears, Grandpa rescued the beetroot and swore in Russian and Tanya's Anatoli was holding two babies and the stuffed cabbage leaves.

Peter the Great was howling underneath the whole disaster and when Uncle Vodka fell on his knees and crawled under to see if he was all right, he got bitten on the nose. 'What did you do that for?' he bellowed.

And Mrs Mudd began to laugh.

Boris stared in astonishment. He had never seen Mrs Mudd laugh. He didn't think she could. But now she laughed until tears ran down her face. 'You lot,' she said, 'you're all hopeless. Completely hopeless. You, Vodka or whatever your name is, get that dog out of there and let me have a look at this table.'

Uncle Vodka and Peter the Great came out, causing another small landslide of the things that were still on the collapsed table. People did some more rescuing, and Mrs Mudd bent down and looked. 'I see,' she said. 'Somebody get me a screwdriver.'

Everyone looked at each other. 'Screwdriver,' Ivan murmured. 'Goodness. Do we have one?'

They didn't, of course.

'Right,' said Mrs Mudd. She disappeared out of the back door, went round to her own house and came back with a handful of useful tools. In a few minutes, she had mended the table, and all the dishes and plates were put back on it. Peter the Great licked up the dribbles of sauce and gravy that were on the floor underneath, and licked Uncle Vodka's hand as well, as if to say he was sorry about accidentally biting him.

*

The meal was absolutely wonderful, and Mrs Mudd ended up wearing a pink-and-orange paper hat out of a cracker, and didn't say a word about headaches.

'Do you like mending things?' asked Boris.

'Yes, I do,' said Mrs Mudd. 'Always did. But this new bungalow they've put me in, there's nothing to mend. All spick and span.'

'There's lots to mend here,' said Boris. 'The doorbell, for a start.'

'I'll be round in the morning,' said Mrs Mudd. 'If that's all right.'

'It's wonderful!' Boris's mother said. 'You don't know how welcome you'll be.'

The music had started up again and to Boris's amazement, Mrs Mudd disappeared round to her house again, returning with a piano accordion that had a zigzag pattern of shiny red and silver. 'I used to play a bit,' she said.

She squeezed out a few chords and then began a rather slow waltz. Ivan joined in on the violin and Anatoli put in a lot of fancy bits on the piano. Then they played something much quicker and everyone danced, even Uncle Vodka and the dog. Masha said she could dance on the table now it was mended – so she did. Altogether, Boris thought, it was the best Christmas he'd ever had.

Afterwards, Mrs Mudd came round quite a lot, and mended things as fast as they broke. She was never what you'd call a really cheerful person, but she laughed from time to time. And she kept them well supplied with Brussels sprouts.

The Story of the Christmas Rose

(A Scandinavian Legend)

Retold by NORAH MONTGOMERIE

Long, long ago there was a Robber family who lived in the Great Forest. Robber Father had stolen sheep and the Bishop had made him an outlaw. So the Robber family went into the forest and there they lived in the shelter of a deep cave, for they had nowhere else to go. Robber Father hunted for food, while Robber Mother and their five children gathered berries to eat, ferns for their beds and wood for the fire.

Sometimes Robber Mother took the children into the village to beg, but they looked so rough and wild with their unkempt hair and their ragged clothes, people were afraid of them and locked their doors when they saw them coming. Sometimes the people left a bundle of old clothes or a parcel of food outside the door for Robber Mother to collect. But not once did they ask her in or even say a word of greeting, as they did to any stranger. This made Robber Mother furious. She scowled and muttered to herself, even when her sack was full, and looked more fierce than ever.

One warm summer day, as she trudged home, her sack slung over her shoulder, Robber Mother saw that a little door in the monastery wall had been left open. She stopped and peeped in. There she saw a beautiful garden filled with bright flowers. Honeysuckle, red roses and white jasmine covered the grey stone walls, and she had never seen so many butterflies. She put down her sack and walked into the garden. She bent down to smell the pink roses and smiled.

You can imagine how surprised the monastery gardener was when he saw the rough Robber Mother in his beautiful garden.

'Hi there!' he shouted. 'You can't come in here, this is the Abbot's private garden. No women are allowed in here. Be off with you!'

Robber Mother looked up and scowled fiercely.

'I'm doing no harm' she snapped, 'and I'll go when I've found what I'm looking for.'

'You'll go right now, my good woman,' shouted the gardener, 'or I'll throw you out!'

'Just you try!' laughed Robber Mother, who was much bigger than the gardener and probably stronger too.

This made the gardener very angry. He went off and fetched two fat monks who tried to put her out. But she bit and kicked and screamed, and made such a noise that the old Abbot came hurrying out to see what all the fuss was about.

'This woman won't leave your garden, Lord Abbot,' said one of the monks.

'Leave her to me, brothers, I will deal with her,' said the Abbot and turning to Robber Mother, he said, 'I expect you have never seen such a fine garden, my good woman. Do you want to pick some of the flowers?'

'I do not,' said Robber Mother. 'This is a fine garden, but it cannot compare with the one we have in the Great Forest every Christmas.'

'Is that so?' laughed the Abbot. His garden was his pride and joy and was said to be the finest in the land. But Robber Mother said angrily:

'I'm not joking, Lord Abbot, I know what I'm saying. Every Christmas Eve, part of the Great Forest near our cave is transformed into a wonderful garden to celebrate the birth of the Christ Child. We who live in the forest see it every year. In that garden flowers of all the seasons grow together at the same time, and there are flowers there I would not dare to touch, they are so beautiful. They have frail silver petals and pale gold stamens. We call them Christmas roses. I do not see them in your garden.'

The old Abbot listened to Robber Mother. He remembered hearing, as a child, how part of the Great Forest was transformed into a beautiful garden on Christmas Eve. He had longed to see it and then he had forgotten all about it. So he smiled kindly at Robber Mother.

'I have heard of your garden,' he said, 'and I would like to see it. Would you send one of your children to guide me to the spot next Christmas Eve?'

'How can we be sure you will not drive us away from our cave if we show you where it is?' said Robber Mother.

'I would not do that,' said the Abbot. 'I would rather ask my Lord Bishop to grant your husband a free pardon in return for your kindness.'

'You would do that?' asked Robber Mother eagerly.

'Yes, I shall ask,' said the old Abbot, 'but whether my Lord Bishop will grant my request I do not know.'

'I trust you,' said Robber Mother, 'and my eldest boy will wait for you next Christmas Eve and guide you through the Great Forest to our cave. He will wait for you by the old oak. But you must promise you will bring only one companion with you – this gardener here.'

'I promise,' said the Abbot, and after he had blessed

the Robber Mother, she left the garden quietly and returned home.

The Abbot went to the Bishop and told him all that had happened, and the story of the Christmas garden. 'If God allows the Robber family to see this miracle there must be some good in them. Will you not give the Robber Father a free pardon and a chance to live and work like our people? As it is, their children are growing up rough and wild. If we are not careful we shall have a young Robber gang up there in the Great Forest, and then there will be trouble.'

'There is some truth in what you say, good father Abbot,' said the Bishop. 'Not that I believe this story of the Christmas garden. However, you can go and look for it if you wish, and if you bring me back one of those silver and gold flowers, I'll grant the Robber a free pardon with pleasure.'

Well, Christmas Eve came at last. The good old Abbot asked his gardener to go with him into the Great Forest, and there, under the old oak, waited the eldest Robber Son. The gardener muttered angrily under his breath as they followed the boy through the dark forest. He had not wanted to leave his warm home on Christmas Eve. He thought of his cosy chair beside the fire, and he wished he was sitting in it, watching his wife pluck the turkey and his children decorate the Christmas tree. He did not believe in the Christmas garden and thought the whole expedition was stupid. However, he dared not disobey his old master and he was too fond of him to do so.

On and on they tramped through the snow till they came to a cave. They followed the boy through an opening into a cavern where the Robber Mother was sitting beside a log fire. The Robber children sprawled about the floor playing with small stones, while Robber Father lay stretched out on a pile of dried bracken.

'Sit down by the fire and warm yourself, Lord Abbot,' said Robber Mother. 'You can sleep if you're tired. I'll keep watch and I'll wake you when it is time to see what you have come to see.'

'I'll keep watch too,' said the gardener, who still did not trust the Robber family.

The old Abbot thanked the woman and stretched himself on the ground beside the fire and fell asleep. He was so tired.

He had not slept long when he woke to hear the chimes of the Christmas bells. The gardener helped him to his feet and they followed the Robber family to the entrance of the cave.

'It is extraordinary to be able to hear the Christmas bells here in the forest. I wouldn't have thought it possible,' said the Abbot.

'Ah well, everything looks the same as ever out here,'

grumbled the gardener, who was still in a bad temper.

It was true, the forest was as dark and gloomy as before, but instead of an icy wind, they felt a warm gentle breeze and a strange stirring all about them. Suddenly the bells stopped ringing. And then it happened.

The darkness turned into a pink dawn. The snow melted from the ground, leaving emerald shoots that grew before their eyes. Ferns sent up their fronds, curled like a bishop's staff, and spring flowers carpeted the earth. Trees burst into leaf and then into blossom. Butterflies and birds darted from tree to tree, and there was a soft hum of insects.

The Robber children laughed and rolled in the grass while Robber Mother and Robber Father stared wide-eyed and smiling. They too seemed transformed. And there, at his feet, the Abbot saw the silver and gold flower of the Christmas rose. He was filled with happiness and he knelt down and thanked God for allowing him to see such a miracle.

This seemed to make the gardener more angry than ever.

'This is no miracle,' he said in a loud voice, 'this is witchcraft and the work of the devil!'

As he said this darkness fell and an icy wind blew snow through the forest. The Robber family ran shivering into the cave, but the old Abbot stumbled forward on his face, clutching at the earth as he fell. The garden vanished, leaving the forest as dark and gloomy as ever.

The gardener hoisted the Abbot on to his back and carried him back to the monastery. There he was laid on his bed. The monks all marvelled at the radiant smile on his still face. At least he had died with a happy heart, they told each other.

Now, the old Abbot was found to have the root of a plant clutched in one hand. It was given to the gardener who planted it carefully in the Abbot's garden. Every day he went to see if it was growing, but although there were green leaves there were no signs of a flower in the spring, nor in the summer, and autumn passed and there was not even a bud to be seen. The gardener wondered if it would ever flower.

Then on Christmas morning, when the ground was sprinkled with snow, the gardener saw a beautiful cluster of silvery white flowers growing from the plant, their frail petals surrounding the pale golden stamens. He had seen the flower only once before, in that Christmas garden of the Great Forest. It must be the Christmas rose, and the good Abbot had managed to pluck one after all.

At once the gardener knew what he must do. He picked three of the white flowers and took them to the Bishop.

'My Lord Bishop,' said the gardener, 'our father Abbot sends you these flowers as he promised.' Then he told the

Bishop about the wonderful Christmas garden and all that had happened in the Great Forest that Christmas Eve.

'The good Abbot kept his promise and I shall keep mine,' said the Bishop, and he wrote a free pardon for the Robber Father there and then.

The gardener took the pardon to the Robber Father but when he reached the cave he found the entrance barred against him.

'Go away!' roared Robber Father. 'Thanks to you there was no wonderful garden here this Christmas Eve. Go away, unless you want a fight!'

'You're right, it was my fault; I had no faith. I was wrong but you must allow me to deliver your free pardon from the Bishop. You are free, and from now on you may return to the village and live and work among the people.'

And so it was that the Robber family left the Great Forest and were able to enjoy Christmas in their own home, with all their friends around them.

Not Just for Christmas

ROB CHILDS

James woke up very early with an extra special sense of excitement.

'Christmas Day!' He felt like shouting it out. He had been looking forward to this day for so long, and now — at last — it was here!

Trembling, James sat up in bed and rubbed his eyes. He opened them again, slowly, but everywhere was dark and he still couldn't see anything.

He tried not to be too disappointed. 'Maybe they're with all my other presents,' he murmured. 'Santa must have been by now.'

James liked to talk to himself, to hear the sound of his voice in the darkness. He was glad he had his own bedroom. It was his private little world, a place where he knew that nobody else would be nearby to listen. Like Hannah, for instance.

His sister was OK to play with at times, he admitted, but she was only five, three years younger than him. Her never-ending chatter often irritated him, especially if she got too big for her boots and tried to do things for him.

'I wonder where everything will be this year?' he said aloud.

It was part of the family fun at Christmas. After Santa's visit, Mum and Dad would hide the presents all over the house and then go back to sleep. He and Hannah had to wait, bursting with anticipation, until their parents said they could start looking. James considered whether he might risk going to wake them up yet so he could begin the hunt.

'Bet it's still a bit too early.'

He reached under the pillows instead for his favourite toy soldier, but his fingers first touched a piece of paper. It was a copy of his letter to Santa, put there for safe keeping, and he gave it a superstitious pat.

Then his hand closed around the small plastic figure with a gun and he whipped it out with a flourish. 'Bang!'

he cried, pretending to shoot at the one-eared teddy bear that lay by his side. 'Bang! Bang!'

He chuckled as Teddy had to dive down on to the carpet to escape the bullets. James leaped out of bed after him and the fight went on as Sam the soldier chased Teddy across the floor.

'Oooh! It's too cold!' James said, with a shiver. He grabbed Teddy and scrambled back under the duvet, wriggling right down until he was completely covered. Snuggling up with Teddy, he felt warm again and happy, hoping it wouldn't be long before he'd be able to see all the pretty lights on the Christmas tree. He closed his eyes and crossed his fingers.

'James! James! Wake up!'

He was being pushed and pulled about, but he stayed underneath the thick duvet out of sight.

'I *am* awake,' came his muffled voice. 'Go away!'

'You were fast asleep,' Hannah insisted. 'I was awake before you.'

His tousled head shot out from the covers. 'No, you weren't. I've been awake for years.'

'No, you haven't! I was up first this morning.'

'Rubbish! I even helped Santa empty his sack!'

Hannah gave up. She could never win such silly arguments with her stubborn big brother.

'It's time!' she announced instead.

James knew exactly what she meant. 'I know,' he replied. 'I was just waiting for you, that's all, so we went in together.'

She gave him a funny look, but knew that all the faces she might pull were just wasted on James. 'Come on then. Let's go in!'

Tingling with excitement, the children crept along the landing and pushed open the door to their parents' bedroom.

'Dad's snoring,' James hissed.

'Goodie!' giggled Hannah. 'We can both sneak up on him and make him jump!'

James felt his sister's hand slide into his as they tiptoed into the room towards Dad's side of the bed.

'Oh no, you don't, you two!' came a voice in the darkness. 'I know what you're up to!'

'Mummy!' Hannah squealed. 'Oh, you spoiled it!'

Mum laughed. 'You little pests. Do you know what time it is?'

'No,' said James, 'but I do know what day it is. It's Christmas Day!'

'Come on in,' Mum invited them, drawing back the duvet covers. 'Come and have a Christmas cuddle.'

Hannah slithered in front for a kiss from Mum, quickly followed by James. Dad rolled over. 'Who's the elephant with cold feet?' he grumbled sleepily.

'James, Daddy!' Hannah cried. 'Happy Christmas!'

'Christmas is cancelled!'

'No, it's not!' they chorused.

'Yes, it is,' he said. 'Haven't you heard? Santa's gone on holiday!'

'No, he hasn't. You're just teasing,' James chuckled, punching Dad on the shoulder. 'He only goes on holiday after he's delivered all our presents. It's time now.'

'It's time, Mummy,' echoed Hannah. 'It's time!'

'I can see we're not going to get any peace,' Mum said. 'OK, it's time. Off you go while I make a drink.'

The children whooped their delight and shot out of the bed, desperate to be the one to find the first present. They always knew whose it was by the wrapping. Hannah's gifts had ribbon around them and a bow, while James's were tied up loosely with string. He loved pulling off the string and tearing open the packaging to see what was inside.

'Found one straight away!' he screamed proudly as he squirmed underneath the bed. 'And it's mine!'

He ripped the string and wrapping paper away from the box and held it up to his nose. 'Hmm, yummy smell! My favourite chocs!'

His next discovery, at the bottom of a wardrobe, didn't have anything round it at all. It didn't need it. James knew what it was as soon as he felt around the shoes and touched it. 'Wow! A football. Thanks!'

Dad laughed. 'Santa would have had a terrible job trying to wrap up a football! He obviously didn't bother.'

James stopped searching for anything else for a while, dribbling the ball around the bedroom with his bare feet and knocking into things as he lost control.

'Hey! Steady on, superstar,' cried Dad, getting out of bed himself at last. 'You'll go and break something and then we'll all be in trouble. Let's wait till we get outside in the garden later.'

Shrieks and squeals from Hannah confirmed her own successes, and the children spent a very happy hour up and down the stairs, poking and probing into cupboards and drawers. James even found a tape of one of his best-loved stories lying in the bath.

'Good job I didn't turn the taps on first,' he grinned.

Mum laughed. 'No danger of you volunteering to have a bath, is there, you mucky pup.'

She caught Dad's eye and they smiled at what she had just said. Mum put down her cup of tea and pulled the two children gently towards her on the sofa.

'Uncle John is coming round later this morning,' she said, giving them both a hug. 'He's bringing along something else for you, although it's not really a Christmas present. It's something even more special.'

Hannah's eyes widened. 'Is it a pony?' she gasped.

Mum shook her head and smiled. 'No guessing allowed. We want it to be a surprise.'

Mum supervised their washing and dressing while Dad prepared some breakfast. 'What time is Uncle John coming?' asked Hannah the moment she trotted into the kitchen.

'Soon,' Dad said. 'You'll have to be patient and play with all your new toys until he gets here.'

'Will we be able to play with what he's bringing?' she persisted.

'Still trying to work out what it can be, aren't you?' he laughed. 'But yes, you'll certainly be able to play with it.'

James was strangely quiet at the table, nibbling at a piece of toast, and Dad attempted to cheer him up. 'How about us two going out to kick your new ball about a bit, eh?'

James nodded, but didn't look up. 'Have I found *all* my presents yet?' he asked instead.

'Not quite,' Mum replied. 'I think there are still a couple of things hidden away.'

'I'll help him look for them,' Hannah piped up.

'No you won't!' cried James. 'I don't need any help. I'll find them when I'm ready.'

Hannah was about to answer him back until Mum shot her a warning glance and she swiftly changed the subject. 'This is the best Christmas ever,' she beamed. 'I've got everything I wanted. Have you, James?'

'Not yet,' he said simply and slid away from the table to play with the toy cars that he'd left near the fire.

When the bell rang, the children rushed to the door, both wanting to be the one to open it. Hannah won the race – as usual.

'Hi, kids!' Uncle John greeted them. 'Merry Christmas, everyone!'

Hannah looked all around for whatever it was that Uncle John was supposed to have with him. There was nothing to be seen.

'Did you like my presents I got Santa to leave for you?' he asked and then laughed at their blank expressions. 'Just like me when I was your age. Too busy opening the boxes to bother with the labels!'

'Uncle John bought you those horrible noisy, electronic games,' Dad explained, slipping his younger brother a wink. 'Typical! He won't be the one who's got to put up with all the din every time you play with them.'

'Oh, thank you, Uncle John!' Hannah said politely as he picked her up to give her a peck on the cheek.

'Thanks, I'll have some fun with that, annoying Dad,' grinned James.

Uncle John acted as though he'd just remembered something. 'Oh, yes, I almost forgot. There's another thing you'll have a lot of fun with, too. I've left it in the car.'

Still carrying Hannah, he led the way out on to the drive, and his niece suddenly let out a shriek. From her high vantage point, she could see into the back of his estate car. 'A puppy! A real puppy!'

She squirmed out of his grasp and ran to the car to stare through the rear window. 'Oh, it's beautiful. It's so cute. What big eyes!'

'It's a *she*,' Uncle John said. 'And she's not so cute when she leaves little puddles all over your carpet and inside your car!'

The children laughed and demanded the car be open so that they could hold the puppy.

'Thanks for looking after her for a couple of days, John,' Mum said. 'Hope she hasn't been too much trouble to you.'

'None at all,' he grinned. 'Apart from the puddles!'

'What is she?' asked James.

'A labrador,' said Dad. 'And she's just seven weeks old.'

James stroked the puppy's short, stubby nose and chin as Hannah cuddled her. 'What shall we call her?' he wondered.

'Actually, she's already got a name,' said Mum. 'It's Misty.'

'Who gave her that?'

'The people at the kennels where she was born.'

James considered it for a moment. 'OK, Misty's a fine name.'

Mum smiled with relief. 'Do you like her?' she asked anxiously.

He nodded. 'I've often wanted a dog to play with.'

'I know, but we weren't quite sure if it would be a good thing,' Dad said. 'Especially after that big dog down the street knocked you over.'

'It wasn't the dog's fault,' James said. 'I must have stepped on its tail or something and hurt it.'

'You cried,' gloated his sister. 'I remember you crying.'

'So?' he demanded. 'You would have done too. You're always crying. It just made me jump, that's all. I didn't know what was happening.'

'Anyway, never mind now, don't argue,' Mum said, prising the puppy out of Hannah's arms. 'Let James hold Misty for a while, darling.'

Hannah looked down at her dress in dismay. 'Oh! I'm all wet!'

Everyone laughed. 'Serves you right for squeezing her so tight,' Dad chuckled.

'Let's take Misty into the back garden and play ball,' said James as Mum led Hannah into the house to change her clothes.

His new football was far too big for the puppy and James kicked a small ball across the lawn instead. It was ideal. The ball made a rattling sound as it rolled along, attracting her attention, and Misty scampered after it with yelps of excitement.

Dad and Uncle John joined in the game, laughing at the puppy's antics. The ball was just the right size for Misty and light enough for her to nose it through the grass in a wayward dribble. Dad passed the rattling ball to James who timed his next kick perfectly, sending it flying into the bushes by the fence.

'Goal!' cried Uncle John. 'Great stuff, James. We'll have you playing for United yet.'

'Rovers!' James corrected him. 'They're the best team in the land.'

The puppy soon grew weary. She squatted on the lawn and then settled down for a nap.

'Dog-tired! Just like the Rovers' players,' joked Uncle John to tease James again about his favourite football team.

Dad carried Misty inside for a drink of water from the shiny metal bowl that his brother had also brought with him. She lapped noisily at the water, spilling most of it on to the kitchen floor.

'Looks like we'll get through a lot of newspapers, soaking up all her messes,' Mum chuckled. 'I just hope Misty realizes what a lucky puppy she is, coming to live with us until she grows up.'

'Till she grows up?' repeated James in alarm. 'What do you mean?'

Mum put her arm around his shoulders and led him through to the lounge, calling Hannah to join them. As the family sat together near the Christmas tree, Misty curled up asleep on the rug in front of the fire.

'Misty doesn't know it yet,' Mum said, 'but when she's older and specially trained, she's going to have a very important job to do.'

'What's that?' James interrupted impatiently, but the answer stunned him into silence.

'She will become a guide dog for a blind person.'

Dad picked up the story. 'But while she's a puppy, she needs to be looked after and loved just like any normal pet. That's where we come in. We've decided to be puppy-walkers.'

'Puppy-walkers!' giggled Hannah. 'What a funny name!'

'Perhaps it is,' Mum smiled, 'because we'll be doing far more than just walking Misty. She'll be one of the family for a whole year.'

'But then has she got to go to somebody else?' asked James.

'I'm afraid so,' Dad answered. 'But we can always take on another puppy after that, if we want to.'

'We thought it might be better this way at first,' Mum explained. 'Just to let you get used to having a dog around the house. See how you get on together.'

'We'll get on just fine,' he said seriously. 'I've never

heard of people being puppy-walkers. It's a good idea.'

James lay down next to the puppy on the rug, stroking her soft fur and gently fondling her large, floppy ears. He was rewarded with little grunts of contentment, almost like purring, and then felt his hand being licked by a rasping, wet tongue.

'Ooh! It tickles!' he chuckled.

Hannah didn't intend to be left out. She wanted to be licked too, and Misty rolled her tongue along the girl's bare arm as far as she could reach, sending Hannah into fits of giggles.

'Misty certainly won't be going short of love and fuss here, I can see that,' Uncle John laughed. 'She's fallen on her feet all right – and she knows it!'

As the puppy dozed, Hannah disappeared to try on her new ballet costume, but James stayed at Misty's side, his hand resting on one of her stretched out legs. 'She feels so warm,' he murmured happily.

'You look wonderful together, lying there,' Mum told him. 'We'll have to take a photo of you both like that.'

There was no chance now. Misty was awake again – and looking for a spot of mischief. She found a willing partner in James, equally eager to play and tumble about.

'Here you are,' said Dad. 'Have one of my old socks to play tug of war with. Dogs love that game.'

'Hope it's a clean one and not too smelly,' laughed

James, who soon felt a determined tugging at the other end of the sock.

'Misty doesn't seem to mind anyway,' Dad grinned.

James let Misty win some of the battles, but she always brought the sock straight back, nudging him to grab hold of it again. Then he decided to throw it away for her to fetch.

The sock landed right on top of the Christmas cake on the table.

'Good job your mum didn't see that!' cried Uncle John, lifting it off quickly and returning it to James. 'Try again.'

He did, and this time it went into the trifle!

'I think you're better at kicking than throwing,' said Uncle John.

The sock came back with a little trace of cream which Misty soon found. She licked her lips with pleasure at the taste.

James played with Misty almost all day in between her frequent snoozes and feeding times. He even forgot to search for his remaining presents until just before bedtime. He wanted Misty to sleep in his bedroom with him as well, but Mum had to be very firm about that.

'She's better off in the kitchen,' Mum said. 'She needs a place of her own at night too, just like you. And I can put plenty of newspaper all over the floor there around her dog basket!'

Mum sat on the side of his bed and read him a story.

'Have you enjoyed having a puppy to play with?' she asked, before saying goodnight.

James nodded several times. 'We're going to have great fun, Misty and me, while she's with us. I can teach her lots of things.'

'Yes, like how to get into all sorts of trouble, no doubt,' Mum laughed. 'And how to get all mucky!'

'Can I have a dog of my own one day?'

'Of course. When you're older. You'll be able to go everywhere together then.'

James grinned. 'I'll call mine Sam.'

'Why Sam?'

James shrugged, unwilling to admit to his soldier's name. 'I just like the sound of it.'

Mum bent over to kiss him and caught sight of a piece of paper sticking out from underneath his pillow. She guessed what it was. James had insisted on having a copy of the letter she'd written to Santa for him. Mum remembered off by heart the words that he'd wanted her to write, but she couldn't resist the temptation to read them again now.

Mum quietly slid the paper away from the pillow without James realizing what she was doing. He lay with a happy, peaceful expression on his face, his eyes closed.

A few silent tears escaped from hers as she read over the short letter:

Dear Santa,

I hope you are well. My name is James and I am eight years old. Please can I have a new pair of eyes at Christmas? I keep bumping into things. I know this will be difficult, but I'm sure you will find a way of doing it somehow.

Thank you very much.

Love James

P.S. It would even be nice to see my pesky little sister as well.

Mum slipped the paper back into place and kissed James again. That lovely picture of him lying cosily beside Misty in the glow of the fire swam into her mind. 'I'm so glad you like your new pair of eyes, my darling,' she whispered.

He smiled and his eyes flickered open, staring up at her blindly.

Author's note:

The Guide Dogs for the Blind Association run puppy-walking schemes in many parts of the country. Families take a puppy, usually a labrador or a golden retriever, into their home to rear as an ordinary pet for the first year of its life. The young dog then goes to stay at a special training centre to learn how to become a guide dog, but a blind person needs to be at least sixteen before they can own one.

Marley's Ghost

(from *A Christmas Carol*)

CHARLES DICKENS

Scrooge took his melancholy dinner in his usual melancholy tavern; and having read all the newspapers, and
beguiled the rest of the evening with his banker's-book,
went home to bed. He lived in chambers which had
once belonged to his deceased partner. They were a
gloomy suite of rooms, in a lowering pile of building
up a yard ... It was old enough now, and dreary
enough, for nobody lived in it but Scrooge, the other
rooms being all let out as offices. The yard was so dark
that even Scrooge, who knew its every stone, was fain to
grope with his hands. The fog and frost so hung about

the black old gateway of the house that it seemed as if the Genius of the Weather sat in mournful meditation on the threshold.

Now, it is a fact that there was nothing at all particular about the knocker on the door, except that it was very large. It is also a fact that Scrooge had seen it night and morning during his whole residence in that place; also that Scrooge had as little of what is called fancy about him as any man in the City of London, even including – which is a bold word – the corporation, aldermen, and livery. Let it also be borne in mind that Scrooge had not bestowed one thought on Marley, since his last mention of his seven-years' dead partner that afternoon. And then let any man explain to me, if he can, how it happened that Scrooge, having his key in the lock of the door, saw in the knocker, without its undergoing any intermediate process of change, not a knocker, but Marley's face.

Marley's face. It was not in impenetrable shadow, as the other objects in the yard were, but had a dismal light about it, like a bad lobster in a dark cellar. It was not angry or ferocious, but looked at Scrooge as Marley used to look: with ghostly spectacles turned up upon its ghostly forehead. The hair was curiously stirred, as if by breath or hot air; and though the eyes were wide open, they were perfectly motionless. That, and its livid colour, made it horrible; but its horror seemed to be in spite of the face and beyond its control, rather than a part of its own expression.

As Scrooge looked fixedly at this phenomenon, it was a knocker again.

To say that he was not startled, or that his blood was not conscious of a terrible sensation to which it had been a stranger from infancy, would be untrue. But he put his hand upon the key he had relinquished, turned it sturdily, walked in, and lighted his candle.

He *did* pause, with a moment's irresolution, before he shut the door; and he *did* look cautiously behind it first, as if he half-expected to be terrified with the sight of Marley's pigtail sticking out into the hall. But there was nothing on the back of the door, except the screws and nuts that held the knocker on, so he said 'Pooh, pooh!' and closed it with a bang.

The sound resounded through the house like thunder. Every room above, and every cask in the wine-merchant's cellars below, appeared to have a separate peal of echoes of its own. Scrooge was not a man to be frightened by echoes. He fastened the door, and walked across the hall, and up the stairs, slowly too, trimming his candle as he went.

You may talk vaguely about driving a coach-and-six up a good old flight of stairs, or through a bad young Act of Parliament; but I mean to say you might have got a hearse up that staircase, and taken it broadwise, with the splinter-bar towards the wall and the door towards the balustrades — and done it easy. There was plenty of width for that, and room to spare; which is perhaps the reason why Scrooge thought he saw a locomotive hearse going on before him in the gloom. Half a dozen gas-lamps out of the streets wouldn't have lighted the entry too well, so you may suppose that it was pretty dark with Scrooge's dip.

Up Scrooge went, not caring a button for that: darkness is cheap, and Scrooge liked it. But before he shut his heavy door, he walked through his rooms to see that all was right. He had just enough recollection of the face to desire to do that.

Sitting-room, bed-room, lumber-room. All as they should be. Nobody under the table, nobody under the sofa; a small fire in the grate; spoon and basin ready; and the little saucepan of gruel (Scrooge had a cold in his head) upon the hob. Nobody under the bed; nobody in the closet; nobody in his dressing-gown, which was hanging up in a suspicious attitude against the wall. Lumber-room as usual. Old fire-guard, old shoes, two fish-baskets, washing-stand on three legs, and a poker.

Quite satisfied, he closed his door, and locked himself in; double-locked himself in, which was not his custom. Thus secured against surprise, he took off his cravat; put on his dressing-gown and slippers, and his night-cap; and sat down before the fire to take his gruel.

It was a very low fire indeed; nothing on such a bitter night. He was obliged to sit close to it, and brood over it, before he could extract the least sensation of warmth from such a handful of fuel. The fire-place was an old one, built by some Dutch merchant long ago, and paved all round with quaint Dutch tiles, designed to illustrate the Scriptures ... hundreds of figures, to attract his thoughts; and yet that face of Marley, seven years dead, came like the ancient Prophet's rod, and swallowed up the whole. If each smooth tile had been a blank at first, with power to shape some picture on its surface from the disjointed fragments of his thoughts, there would have been a copy of old Marley's head on every one.

'Humbug!' said Scrooge, and walked across the room.

After several turns, he sat down again. As he threw his head back in the chair, his glance happened to rest upon a bell, a disused bell, that hung in the room, and communicated for some purpose now forgotten with a chamber in the highest storey of the building. It was with great astonishment, and with a strange, inexplicable dread, that as he looked, he saw this bell begin to swing. It swung so softly in the outset that it scarcely made a sound; but soon it rang out loudly, and so did every bell in the house.

This might have lasted half a minute, or a minute, but

it seemed an hour. The bells ceased as they had begun, together. They were succeeded by a clanking noise, deep down below; as if some person were dragging a heavy chain over the casks in the wine-merchant's cellar. Scrooge then remembered to have heard that ghosts in haunted houses were described as dragging chains.

The cellar-door flew open with a booming sound, and then he heard the noise much louder, on the floors below; then coming up the stairs; then coming straight towards his door.

'It's humbug still!' said Scrooge. 'I won't believe it.'

His colour changed though, when, without a pause, it came on through the heavy door, and passed into the room before his eyes. Upon its coming in, the dying flame leaped up, as though it cried 'I know him! Marley's Ghost!' and fell again.

The same face: the very same. Marley in his pigtail, usual waistcoat, tights, and boots; the tassels on the latter bristling, like his pigtail, and his coat-skirts, and the hair upon his head. The chain he drew was clasped about his middle. It was long, and wound about him like a tail; and it was made (for Scrooge observed it closely) of cash-boxes, keys, padlocks, ledgers, deeds, and heavy purses wrought in steel. His body was transparent, so that Scrooge, observing him, and looking through his waistcoat, could see the two buttons on his coat behind.

Scrooge had often heard it said that Marley had no bowels, but he had never believed it until now.

No, nor did he believe it even now. Though he looked the phantom through and through, and saw it standing before him; though he felt the chilling influence of its death-cold eyes; and marked the very texture of the folded kerchief bound about its head and chin, which wrapper he had not observed before; he was still incredulous, and fought against his senses.

'How now!' said Scrooge, caustic and cold as ever. 'What do you want with me?'

'Much!' – Marley's voice, no doubt about it.

'Who are you?'

'Ask me who I *was*.'

'Who *were* you then?' said Scrooge, raising his voice. 'You're particular – for a shade.' He was going to say '*to* a shade,' but substituted this, as more appropriate.

'In life I was your partner, Jacob Marley.'

'Can you – can you sit down?' asked Scrooge, looking doubtfully at him.

'I can.'

'Do it then.'

Scrooge asked the question, because he didn't know whether a ghost so transparent might find himself in a condition to take a chair; and felt that in the event of its being impossible, it might involve the necessity of an embarrassing explanation. But the ghost sat down on the opposite side of the fire-place, as if he were quite used to it.

'You don't believe in me,' observed the Ghost.

'I don't,' said Scrooge.

'What evidence would you have of my reality beyond that of your senses?'

'I don't know,' said Scrooge.

'Why do you doubt your senses?'

'Because,' said Scrooge, 'a little thing affects them. A slight disorder of the stomach makes them cheats. You may be an undigested bit of beef, a blot of mustard, a crumb of cheese, a fragment of an underdone potato. There's more of gravy than of grave about you, whatever you are!'

Scrooge was not much in the habit of cracking jokes, nor did he feel, in his heart, by any means waggish then. The truth is that he tried to be smart, as a means of distracting his own attention, and keeping down his terror; for the spectre's voice disturbed the very marrow in his bones . . .

'You see this toothpick?' said Scrooge . . .

'I do,' replied the Ghost.

'You are not looking at it,' said Scrooge.

'But I see it,' said the Ghost, 'notwithstanding.'

'Well!' returned Scrooge. 'I have but to swallow this, and

be for the rest of my days persecuted by a legion of goblins, all of my own creation. Humbug, I tell you; humbug!'

At this, the spirit raised a frightful cry, and shook its chain with such a dismal and appalling noise that Scrooge held on tight to his chair, to save himself from falling in a swoon. But how much greater was his horror when the phantom, taking off the bandage round its head, as if it were too warm to wear in-doors, its lower jaw dropped down upon its breast!

Scrooge fell upon his knees, and clasped his hands before his face.

'Mercy!' he said. 'Dreadful apparition, why do you trouble me?'

'Man of the worldly mind,' replied the Ghost, 'do you believe in me or not?'

'I do,' said Scrooge. 'I must. But why do spirits walk the earth, and why do they come to me?'

'It is required of every man,' the Ghost returned, 'that the spirit within him should walk abroad among his fellow-men, and travel far and wide; and if that spirit goes not forth in life, it is condemned to do so after death. It is doomed to wander through the world — oh, woe is me! — and witness that it cannot share, but might have shared on earth, and turned to happiness!'

Again the spectre raised a cry, and shook its chain, and wrung its shadowy hands.

'You are fettered,' said Scrooge, trembling. 'Tell me why?'

'I wear the chain I forged in life,' replied the Ghost. 'I made it link by link, and yard by yard; I girded it on of my own free will, and of my own free will I wore it. Is its pattern strange to *you*?'

Scrooge trembled more and more.

'Or would you know,' pursued the Ghost, 'the weight and length of the strong coil you bear yourself? It was full as heavy and as long as this, seven Christmas Eves ago. You have laboured on it, since. It is a ponderous chain!'

Scrooge glanced about him on the floor, in the expectation of finding himself surrounded by some fifty or sixty fathoms of iron cable; but he could see nothing.

'Jacob,' he said, imploringly. 'Old Jacob Marley, tell me more. Speak comfort to me, Jacob.'

'I have none to give,' the Ghost replied. 'It comes from other regions, Ebenezer Scrooge, and is conveyed by other ministers, to other kinds of men. Nor can I tell you what I would. A very little more is all permitted to me. I cannot rest, I cannot stay, I cannot linger anywhere. My spirit never walked beyond our counting-house – mark me! – in life my spirit never roved beyond the narrow limits of our money-changing hole; and weary journeys lie before me!'

It was a habit with Scrooge, whenever he became thoughtful, to put his hands in his breeches pockets. Pondering on what the Ghost had said, he did so now, but without lifting up his eyes, or getting off his knees . . .

'But you were always a good man of business, Jacob,' faltered Scrooge, who now began to apply this to himself.

'Business!' cried the Ghost, wringing his hands again. 'Mankind was my business. The common welfare was my business; charity, mercy, forbearance and benevolence were, all, my business. The dealings of my trade were but a drop of water in the comprehensive ocean of my business!'

It held up its chain at arm's length, as if that were the cause of all its unavailing grief, and flung it heavily upon the ground again.

'At this time of the rolling year,' the spectre said, 'I suffer most. Why did I walk through crowds of fellow-beings with my eyes turned down, and never raise them to that blessed Star which led the Wise Men to a poor abode? Were there no poor homes to which its light would have conducted *me*!'

Scrooge was very much dismayed to hear the spectre going on at this rate, and began to quake exceedingly.

'Hear me!' cried the Ghost. 'My time is nearly gone.'

'I will,' said Scrooge. 'But don't be hard upon me! Don't be flowery, Jacob! Pray!'

'How it is that I appear before you in a shape that you

can see, I may not tell. I have sat invisible beside you many and many a day.'

It was not an agreeable idea. Scrooge shivered, and wiped the perspiration from his brow.

'There is no light part of my penance,' pursued the Ghost. 'I am here tonight to warn you that you have yet a chance and hope of escaping my fate. A chance and hope of my procuring, Ebenezer.'

'You were always a good friend to me,' said Scrooge. 'Thank'ee!'

'You will be haunted,' resumed the Ghost, 'by Three Spirits.'

Scrooge's countenance fell almost as low as the Ghost's had done.

'Is that the chance and hope you mentioned, Jacob?' he demanded, in a faltering voice.

'It is.'

'I – I think I'd rather not,' said Scrooge.

'Without their visits,' said the Ghost, 'you cannot hope to shun the path I tread. Expect the first tomorrow, when the bell tolls One.'

'Couldn't I take 'em all at once, and have it over, Jacob?' hinted Scrooge.

'Expect the second on the next night at the same hour. The third upon the next night when the last stroke of Twelve has ceased to vibrate. Look to see no more; and look that, for your own sake, you remember what has passed between us!'

When it had said these words, the spectre took its wrapper from the table and bound it round its head, as before. Scrooge knew this, by the smart sound its teeth made, when the jaws were brought together by the bandage. He ventured to raise his eyes again, and found his supernatural visitor confronting him in an erect attitude, with its chain wound over and about its arm.

The apparition walked backward from him; and at every step it took, the window raised itself a little, so that when the spectre reached it, it was wide open. It beckoned Scrooge to approach, which he did. When they were within two paces of each other, Marley's Ghost held up its hand, warning him to come no nearer. Scrooge stopped.

Not so much in obedience, as in surprise and fear: for on the raising of the hand, he became sensible of confused noises in the air; incoherent sounds of lamentation and regret; wailings inexpressibly sorrowful and self-accusatory. The spectre, after listening for a moment, joined in the mournful dirge; and floated out upon the bleak, dark night.

Scrooge followed to the window, desperate in his curiosity. He looked out.

The air was filled with phantoms, wandering hither and thither in restless haste, and moaning as they went. Every one of them wore chains like Marley's Ghost; some few (they might be guilty governments) were linked together; none were free. Many had been personally known to Scrooge in their lives. He had been quite familiar with one old ghost in a white waistcoat, with a monstrous iron safe attached to its ankle, who cried piteously at being unable to assist a wretched woman with an infant, whom it saw below, upon a doorstep. The misery with them all was, clearly, that they sought to interfere, for good, in human matters, and had lost the power for ever.

Whether these creatures faded into mist, or mist enshrouded them, he could not tell. But they and their spirit voices faded together; and the night became as it had been when he walked home.

Scrooge closed the window, and examined the door by which the Ghost had entered. It was double-locked, as he had locked it with his own hands, and the bolts were undisturbed. He tried to say 'Humbug!' but stopped at the first syllable. And being, from the emotion he had undergone, or the fatigues of the day, or his glimpse of the Invisible World, or the dull conversation of the Ghost, or the lateness of the hour, much in need of repose, went straight to bed, without undressing, and fell asleep upon the instant.

Simon and the Snow

GINO ALBERTI

Simon lived in a little house high up in the mountains. It was winter and he was happy, for of all the seasons he loved winter the best.

He loved the snowflakes and the icicles; he loved to take long rides on his sledge, and most of all he loved to build jolly round snowmen with carrot noses.

One day Simon looked around him and noticed grass growing and new buds on the trees. Spring had come early.

Simon was sad: he wished it could be winter for ever.

But that night, as Simon lay sleeping, the air turned cold again. Softly, it began to snow.

The garden was covered in white and the windows were speckled with frost.

As soon as Simon woke up, he noticed that something was different.

He ran to the window and looked out in wonder at the snow. The winter had come back again! It was as if his wish had come true.

'The snow is back! The snow is back!' he cried out joyfully. He put on his woolly hat and mittens and ran outside. He began to build a whole family of snowmen. His mother gave him some carrots for the noses and some straw for the arms. Simon was very happy.

The next day was even colder. As soon as he was up, Simon went to play with his snow family. But what had happened? He ran from one snowman to the next. The twig arms and the carrot noses were gone! Who could have done such a thing?

There was no time to think for Simon's mother was calling him in to breakfast. Later, as Simon fetched some new noses and arms from the kitchen, he made a plan.

That night the sky was so clear you could count the stars. While his mother slept, Simon wrapped up warmly, collected his cat Mutz and climbed out through the window. Together they trudged through the snow until they came to a very tall tree. 'Here's a good place,' said Simon as he climbed up. Mutz followed. They were cold and frightened, but even if they had to stay up all night they would catch the carrot thieves.

For a long, long while everything was still. Then, suddenly, Simon saw something move. Gathering up his courage he climbed down the tree and hid behind a snowman. He could hardly believe his eyes – all kinds of animals were coming out of the forest and they were greedily eating everything they could from the snowmen.

Simon could see that the poor animals were very thin and hungry. The return of the winter had buried their food under deep snow. He quietly took a couple of steps towards them, but the animals ran away in fright.

Later that morning, Simon told his mother what had happened. 'The poor animals are starving,' she said, and she gave him a basket of hay to take to them.

Simon carried the basket to the edge of the forest. The animals gazed at him hungrily. 'Don't be frightened,' Simon whispered.

Very, very slowly a little deer dared to come forward. Then, when the other animals saw it was safe, they too came out of the forest. There were fawns and rabbits and stags and birds. Simon fed as many as he could, but there wasn't enough food for everyone. Then Simon had an idea.

He put the basket on his back and set off to the village. Shyly, the animals followed him. The village people stopped what they were doing to watch the strange little procession making its way down the mountain.

Everyone wanted to hear Simon's story. He told them about his snowmen and how he had discovered the hungry animals. The whole village wanted to help. At the entrance to the village the grown-ups built a big feeding trough. Then all the children ran home to fetch food for the animals.

Every day, the children brought new supplies. There was enough for all.

Soon the snow melted and the days began to grow warmer. The smell of new grass was in the air again. Spring had come at last – this time to stay. The animals could go back to the forest for good.

From that time on, Simon still loved the winter, but now he loved the spring as well, for he knew the importance of the seasons.

Baboushka

Retold by CAITLIN MATTHEWS

Many years ago, in the land of Russia, there lived a woman called Baboushka. Her house was the most beautifully kept in the whole village. From the brightly coloured gables on her wooden roof, right down to her neat little garden, her house was a sight to behold.

Although she lived alone, Baboushka was forever washing and cleaning, baking and cooking, painting and gardening, as if she was expecting a special guest. Although she was past the age of motherhood, she especially loved children and she spent the long, cold winter months making fine little toys. Her hands were clever and strong, and her heart was pure and generous. Everyone in the village was very fond of her.

One evening, in the great expanse of the heavens, there appeared an enormous star with a trailing tail that moved across the sky. Everyone in the village was very excited about the new star, wondering what it could mean, but Baboushka merely smiled and shook her head. 'Whatever it means, there is still the floor to be washed and the bread to be baked.'

But the very next day, the meaning became plain. Over the hills beyond the village came a procession of strangers. They had come from very far off. In the procession were three mighty kings. There was bearded Caspar in his crown of gold, riding upon a high-stepping black horse. There was Melchior in his robes of white, fastened by a jewel shaped like a star, riding upon a fine camel. And there was Balthasar in his gold and red tunic, seated upon a magnificent white stallion. Each of the kings carried a special treasure.

The kings' servants rode down into the village to find lodgings. They sought out the headman and asked him which house was most fitting for their royal masters to sleep throughout that day, for the kings could travel only by night. The headman longed to invite these grand visitors to his own house, but he knew that it was too small and not fine enough. He had fourteen children and the house was often noisy and not always as clean as it might be. So he said to the servants, 'Tell your royal masters to ask at the house with the coloured gables.'

The kings dismounted outside Baboushka's house and knocked on the door. 'Good woman,' they said as she opened the door, 'we need to rest here this day until the star once more appears in the sky. Do we have your leave to enter?'

Baboushka pressed her hands to her cheeks in astonishment, 'Sirs, please come in. You are most welcome!'

Soon the three kings were sitting at her table and enjoying a meal of freshly cooked bread, beetroot soup, pickled herrings and vegetables, all washed down with birch-sap beer.

When they had eaten, Baboushka invited them to sit around her fire and tell her about their journey.

'We are following the star whose glory has been foretold by my people for many years,' said Melchior, the firelight playing upon the starry jewel at his breast.

'Where does it lead?' asked Baboushka.

Caspar spoke from the depths of his beard. 'We believe that the star will lead us to a king who is about to be born.'

Balthasar's dark eyes flashed. 'A king who is King of all the Universe. And we have brought him gifts.'

Baboushka's eyes fell upon the precious things that the

kings had brought with them, and her heart was strangely moved. If these great kings from countries far away thought it important enough to leave their kingdoms to find a humble newborn baby, then that child must be King indeed. If he were greater than they, then he was her King too.

'I wish I could bring him a present,' she said, almost to herself.

'Then why don't you come with us?' suggested Balthasar.

Baboushka looked up, startled, not realizing that she had uttered her wish aloud.

While they slept soundly, Baboushka cleaned away the meal and tidied up the house. So many guests had left her with much more work than usual. Could she really leave home and travel with the three kings? What should she take as a gift? What things would she need for the journey?

At twilight, she wakened the sleeping kings, who made ready to leave. Balthasar stretched out his hand to include her in their procession. 'Are you coming, Baboushka?'

'I have to find a gift. There is so much to get ready. I must tidy the house before I go. I will catch you up.'

The kings went on their way, following the star.

When she looked up and saw the star with her own eyes, Baboushka knew that she really had to go. She rushed back into the house and began to look through her store of gifts. There were wooden animals, carved and painted; there were birch-bark boxes filled with ribbons, polished stones and sweets; there were nesting dolls that sat inside each other; there were whistles made of reeds. Which would be good enough for a newborn king?

Baboushka simply could not decide which was best, so she packed all of them in a big basket. She could make her decision as she travelled, or else create something lovely along the way. By the time she had found her knife and paints, her scissors and threads, and packed them away with her own few things for the journey, she heard the sound of the cockerel crowing that dawn was coming. She gave a great big yawn. How tired she was! She had been awake for a day and a night without sleep and now she fell into a deep slumber.

Baboushka woke up at twilight and rushed out with her basket, keeping the glorious star ever before her. In every village, she asked after the three kings and which way they had gone.

Wherever she asked, people would direct her on to the next village or town, pointing the way that the star was travelling. Baboushka trudged onwards for days and months until she came to the royal palace of Jerusalem.

'At last! This must be where the newborn king will be found,' Baboushka thought. She asked a guard outside the walls but he said, 'Yes, the three kings came here but they soon departed, hurrying onwards to a poor little place called Bethlehem.'

Off she went at once. She arrived at twilight and saw how the great star seemed to be directly overhead. Her heart leaped. This must be the place! At the inn she asked the innkeeper, 'Have the three kings been here?'

'Yes. They came to see the baby that was born in the stable here. But the kings have gone home now.'

'And the baby?' asked Baboushka, with a trembling voice.

'Oh, the baby and his family went away as well — to Egypt, I think,' said the innkeeper. Then, seeing her disappointment, he added, 'I can show you the place where the baby was, if you like?'

Baboushka raised tear-filled eyes and followed him to the stable behind the inn. It was like a dimly lit cave inside. 'There is where his mother laid him, in the straw of the manger,' said the innkeeper. 'Who would have thought that the Christ-child, Jesus, would be born in my stable?'

When Baboushka heard the baby's name, she fell on her knees. Peering into the straw, she raised some of it to her face and kissed it. She barely heard the innkeeper telling her about the visit of the shepherds who had heard the message of angels, or about the presentation of gifts by the three kings.

At the thought of the gift that she wanted to give the Christ-child, Baboushka rose and thanked the innkeeper.

'I'm going to find him, King Jesus, and give him my gift,' she said.

And, from that day to this, Baboushka journeys on with her basket of toys, asking everywhere she goes for the newborn king. At every house, especially at Christmas, she looks at the children asleep in their beds and leaves a toy, just in case it might be the King of her heart.

Acknowledgements

The editor and publishers gratefully acknowledge the following, for permission to reproduce copyright material for this anthology. Every effort has been made to trace copyright holders but in a few cases this has proved impossible. The editor and publishers apologize for these cases of copyright transgression and would like to hear from any copyright holder not acknowledged.

'The Christmas Party' by George Layton from *A Northern Childhood*, published in *The Balaclava Boys and Other Stories*, published by The Longman Group UK Limited 1976, copyright © George Layton 1976, reprinted by permission of Pearson Education Limited. 'The Silver Horse' by Ursula Moray Williams from *Time for a Story*, edited by Eileen Colwell, published by Puffin Books 1967, copyright © Ursula Moray Williams 1967, reproduced by permission of Curtis Brown Limited, London, on behalf of Ursula Moray Williams. 'Just Like an Angel' by Gillian Cross from *Wondrous Christmas Stories*, edited by Anne Finnis, published by Scholastic Limited 1997, copyright © Gillian Cross 1997, reprinted by permission of Scholastic Limited. 'The Real Father Christmas' by Kate Petty from *It's Christmas*, edited by Wendy Cooling, published by Orion Children's Books 1997, copyright © Kate Petty 1997, reprinted by permission of The Orion Publishing Group Limited. 'Why the Chimes Rang' by Raymond MacDonald Alden, reprinted with permission from *A Classic Christmas Treasury*, illustrated by Christian Birmingham, copyright © 1997 by Running Press. First published in the United States by Courage Books, an imprint of Running Press Book Publishers, Philadelphia and London. First published in Great Britain by Harper-Collins Publishers Limited, London. 'Little Brown Jesus' by Joan O'Donovan from *Shadows on the Wall*, published by Victor Gollancz 1960, copyright © Joan O'Donovan 1960. 'The Box of Magic' by Malorie Blackman from *Magical Christmas Stories*, edited by Anne Finnis, published by Scholastic Limited 1995, copyright © Malorie Blackman 1995, reprinted by permission of Scholastic Limited. 'Christmas Is Coming' by Alison Uttley from *The Country Child*, copyright © Alison Uttley 1931, reprinted by permission of The Alison Uttley Literary Property Trust. 'Schnitzle, Schnotzle and Schnootzle' by Ruth Sawyer from *The Long Christmas*, by Ruth Sawyer, copyright © Ruth Sawyer 1941, Reprinted by permission of Viking Penguin, an imprint of Penguin Putnam Books for Young Readers, a division of Penguin Putnam Inc. 'Mrs Mudd's Cross Christmas' by Alison Prince from *It's Christmas*, edited by Wendy Cooling, published by Orion Children's Books 1997, copyright © Alison Prince 1997, reprinted by permission of The Orion Publishing Group Limited. 'Not Just for Christmas' by Rob Childs from *Wondrous Christmas Stories* edited by Anne Finnis, published by Scholastic Limited, copyright © Rob Childs, reprinted by permission of Celia Catchpole. 'Simon and the Snow' by Gino Alberti from *Once Upon a Christmas Time*, published by Hutchinson, copyright © Gino Alberti. Used by permission of The Random House Group Limited. 'Baboushka' retold by Caitlín Matthews from *While the Bear Sleeps: Winter Tales and Traditions*, reprinted by permission of Barefoot Books Limited, copyright © 1999 Caitlín Matthews.